LADY SUSAN

JANE AUSTEN

DOVER PUBLICATIONS, INC.
MINEOLA, NEW YORK

Copyright

Copyright © 2005 by Dover Publications, Inc.
All rights reserved.

Bibliographical Note

This Dover edition, first published in 2005, is an unabridged republica-
tion of the work as first published in J. E. Austen Leigh's *A Memoir of Jane
Austen* (i.e., the second edition, published in 1871 by Richard Bentley and
Son, London), and other standard editions. The Introduction, "Portrait of
Jane Austen," is comprised of excerpts from Austen Leigh's *Memoir*.

Lady Susan was written about 1805, but was published for the first time
in 1871; the occasional misspellings and minor inconsistencies that derive
from the original have been retained here for the sake of authenticity.

Library of Congress Cataloging-in-Publication Data

Austen, Jane, 1775–1817.
    Lady Susan / Jane Austen.
      p. cm.
    ISBN-13: 978-0-486-44407-9 (pbk.)
    ISBN-10: 0-486-44407-4 (pbk.)
    1. Widows—Fiction. 2. England—Fiction. 3. Mate selection—
Fiction. 4. Mothers and daughters—Fiction. I. Title.

PR4034.L3 2005
823'.7—dc22

2005049221

Manufactured in the United States by RR Donnelley
44407407   2016
www.doverpublications.com

PORTRAIT OF JANE AUSTEN[1]

J. E. Austen Leigh

Jane Austen was born on December 16, 1775, at the Parsonage House of Steventon in Hampshire. Her father, the Rev. George Austen, was of a family long established in the neighborhood of Tenterden and Sevenoaks in Kent. Mr. Austen was a remarkably good-looking man, both in his youth and his old age. Being a good scholar he was able to prepare two of his sons for the University, and to direct the studies of his other children, whether sons or daughters, as well as to increase his income by taking pupils. In Mrs. Austen also was to be found much of the ability which was concentrated in Jane, but of which others of her children had a share. She united strong common sense with a lively imagination, and often expressed herself, both in writing and in conversation, with epigrammatic force and point.

Of events Jane's life was singularly barren: few changes and no great crisis ever broke the smooth current of its course. Even her fame may be said to have been posthumous: it did not attain to any vigorous life till she had ceased to exist. Her talents did not introduce her to the notice of other writers, or connect her with the literary world, or in any degree pierce through the obscurity of her domestic retirement. Her own family were so much, and the rest of the world so little, to Jane Austen.

---

[1] The Portrait is comprised of excerpts from *A Memoir of Jane Austen* by her nephew J. E. Austen Leigh (Richard Bentley and Son, London, 1871). The work is the only published biography of Austen by someone who knew her. The use of ellipsis to denote excised text has been dispensed with for the sake of a better narrative flow, since the piece includes passages from numerous chapters throughout the book. A very few liberties have also been taken with respect to the chronological arrangement of the text for the same reason. [ED.]

Dearest of all to the heart of Jane was her sister Cassandra,[2] about three years her senior. Their sisterly affection for each other could scarcely be exceeded. This attachment was never interrupted or weakened. They lived in the same home, and shared the same bed-room, till separated by death. They were not exactly alike. Cassandra's was the colder and calmer disposition; she was always prudent and well judging, but with less outward demonstration of feeling and less sunniness of temper than Jane possessed. It was remarked in her family that "Cassandra had the *merit* of having her temper always under command, but that Jane had the *happiness* of a temper that never required to be commanded."

The family talk had abundance of spirit and vivacity, and was never troubled by disagreements even in little matters, for it was not their habit to dispute or argue with each other: above all, there was strong family affection and firm union, never to be broken but by death. It cannot be doubted that all this had its influence on the author in the construction of her stories, in which a family party usually supplies the narrow stage, while the interest is made to revolve around a few actors.

It will be seen also that though her circle of society was small, yet she found in her neighborhood persons of good taste and cultivated minds. Her acquaintance, in fact, constituted the very class from which she took her imaginary characters, ranging from the member of parliament, or large landed proprietor, to the young curate or younger midshipman of equally good family; and I think that the influence of these early associations may be traced in her writings, especially in two particulars. First, that she is entirely free from the vulgarity, which is so offensive in some novels, of dwelling on the outward appendages of wealth or rank, as if they were things to which the writer was unaccustomed; and, secondly, that she deals as little with very low as with very high stations in life.

As the first twenty-five years, more than half of the brief life

---

[2] Austen was the seventh of eight children; in addition to her sister, she had six brothers. [ED.]

of Jane Austen, were spent in the parsonage of Steventon, some description of that place ought to be given. Steventon is a small rural village upon the chalk hills of north Hants, situated in a winding valley about seven miles from Basingstoke. The house itself stood in a shallow valley, surrounded by sloping meadows, well sprinkled with elm trees, at the end of a small village of cottages, each provided with a garden, scattered about prettily on either side of the road. It was sufficiently commodious to hold pupils in addition to a growing family, and was in those times considered to be above the average of parsonages; but the rooms were finished with less elegance than would now be found in the most ordinary dwellings. But the chief beauty of Steventon consisted in its hedgerows. A hedgerow, in that country, does not mean a thin formal line of quickset, but an irregular border of copse-wood and timber, often wide enough to contain within it a winding footpath, or a rough cart track. Under its shelter the earliest primroses, anemones, and wild hyacinths were to be found; sometimes, the first bird's-nest; and, now and then, the unwelcome adder. But whatever may be the beauties or defects of the surrounding scenery, this was the residence of Jane Austen for twenty-five years. This was the cradle of her genius. The home at Steventon must have been, for many years, a pleasant and prosperous one. The family was unbroken by death, and seldom visited by sorrow.

In childhood every available opportunity of instruction was made use of. According to the ideas of the time, Jane was well educated, though not highly accomplished, and she certainly enjoyed that important element of mental training, associating at home with persons of cultivated intellect. To these sources of enjoyment must be added the first stirrings of talent within her, and the absorbing interest of original composition. It is impossible to say at how early an age she began to write. There are copy books extant containing tales some of which must have been composed while she was a young girl, as they had amounted to a considerable number by the time she was sixteen. Her earliest stories are of a slight and flimsy texture, and are generally intended to be nonsensical, but the nonsense has much spirit in it. Perhaps the most characteristic feature in these early productions is that, however puerile the matter, they are always composed in pure simple English, quite free from the over-ornamented style which might be expected from so young a writer.

During this preparatory period her mind seems to have been working in a very different direction from that into which it ultimately settled. Instead of presenting faithful copies of nature, these tales were generally burlesques, ridiculing the improbable events and exaggerated sentiments which she had met with in sundry silly romances. It would seem as if she were first taking note of all the faults to be avoided, and curiously considering how she ought *not* to write before she attempted to put forth her strength in the right direction.

It was at Steventon that the real foundations of her fame were laid. There some of her most successful writing was composed at such an early age as to make it surprising that so young a woman could have acquired the insight into character, and the nice observation of manners which they display. *Pride and Prejudice,* which some consider the most brilliant of her novels, was the first finished, if not the first begun. She began it in October 1796, before she was twenty-one years old, and completed it in about ten months, in August 1797. The title then intended for it was *First Impressions. Sense and Sensibility* was begun, in its present form, immediately after the completion of the former, in November 1797; but something similar in story and character had been written earlier under the title of *Elinor and Marianne*; and if, as is probable, a good deal of this earlier production was retained, it must form the earliest specimen of her writing that has been given to the world. *Northanger Abbey,* though not prepared for the press till 1803, was certainly first composed in 1798.

The family removed to Bath in the spring of 1801, where they resided first at No. 4 Sydney Terrace, and afterwards in Green Park Buildings. I do not know whether they were at all attracted to Bath by the circumstance that Mrs. Austen's only brother, Mr. Leigh Perrot, spent part of every year there. The unfinished story, now published under the title of *The Watsons,* must have been written during the author's residence in Bath. In February 1805, her father died at Bath, and was buried at Walcot Church. The only records that I can find about her during those four years are three letters to her sister; one from Lyme, the others from Bath. They shew that she went a good deal into society, in a quiet way, chiefly with ladies; and that her eyes were always open to minute traits of character in those with whom she associated.

Before the end of 1805, the little family party removed to Southampton. They resided in a commodious old-fashioned house in a corner of Castle Square. In 1809, the mother and daughters settled themselves in Chawton Cottage [Hampshire], the *second,* as well as the *last* home of Jane Austen; for during the temporary residences of the party at Bath and Southampton she was only a sojourner in a strange land; but here she found a real home amongst her own people. It so happened that during her residence at Chawton circumstances brought several of her brothers and their families within easy distance of the house. Chawton must also be considered the place most closely connected with her career as a writer; for there it was that, in the maturity of her mind, she either wrote or rearranged, and prepared for publication the books by which she has become known to the world. This was the home where, after a few years, while still in the prime of her life, she began to droop and wither away, and which she left only in the last stage of her illness, yielding to the persuasion of friends hoping against hope.

As my memoir has now reached the period when I saw a great deal of my aunt, and was old enough to understand something of her value, I will here attempt a description of her person, mind, and habits. In person she was very attractive; her figure was rather tall and slender, her step light and firm, and her whole appearance expressive of health and animation. In complexion she was a clear brunette with a rich color; she had full round cheeks, with mouth and nose small and well formed, bright hazel eyes, and brown hair forming natural curls close round her face. At the time of which I am now writing, she never was seen, either morning or evening, without a cap; I believe that she and her sister were generally thought to have taken to the garb of middle age earlier than their years or their looks required; and that, though remarkably neat in their dress as in all their ways, they were scarcely sufficiently regardful of the fashionable, or the becoming.

Jane did not pass through life without being the object of warm affection. In her youth she had declined the addresses of a gentleman who had the recommendations of good character, and connections, and position in life, of everything, in fact, except the subtle power of touching her heart. There is, however, one passage of romance in her history with which I am imperfectly acquainted, and to which I am unable to assign name, or date, or place, though I have it on sufficient authority. Many years after her death, some circumstances induced her sister Cassandra to break through her habitual reticence, and to speak of it. She said that, while staying at some seaside place, they became acquainted with a gentleman, whose charm of person, mind, and manners was such that Cassandra thought him worthy to possess and likely to win her sister's love. When they parted, he expressed his intention of soon seeing them again; and Cassandra felt no doubt as to his motives. But they never again met. Within a short time they heard of his sudden death. I believe that, if Jane ever loved, it was this unnamed gentleman; but the acquaintance had been short, and I am unable to say whether her feelings were of such a nature as to affect her happiness.

Jane was not highly accomplished according to the present standard. She was fond of music, and had a sweet voice, both in singing and in conversation; in her youth she had received some instruction on the pianoforte; and at Chawton she practised daily, chiefly before breakfast. She read French with facility, and knew something of Italian. In history she followed the old guides—Goldsmith, Hume, and Robertson. Jane, when a girl, had strong political opinions, especially about the affairs of the sixteenth and seventeenth centuries. She was a vehement defender of Charles I and his grandmother Mary; but I think it was rather from an impulse of feeling than from any enquiry into the evidences by which they must be condemned or acquitted. As she grew up, the politics of the day occupied very little of her attention, but she probably shared the feeling of moderate Toryism which prevailed in her family.

She was well acquainted with the old periodicals from the *Spectator* downwards. Her knowledge of Richardson's works was such as no one is likely again to acquire, now that the multitude and the merits of our light literature have called off the attention of our readers from that great master. Amongst her favorite writers, Johnson in prose, Crabbe in verse, and Cowper in both, stood high. She thoroughly enjoyed Crabbe; perhaps on account of a certain resemblance to herself in minute and highly finished detail; and would sometimes say, in jest, that, if she ever married at all, she could fancy being Mrs. Crabbe; looking on the author quite as an abstract idea, and ignorant and regardless what manner of man he might be. Scott's poetry gave her great pleasure; she did not live to make much acquaintance with his novels.

It may seem extraordinary that Jane Austen should have written so little during the years that elapsed between leaving Steventon and settling at Chawton; especially when this cessation from work is contrasted with her literary activity both before and after that period. It might rather have been expected that fresh scenes and new acquaintance would have called forth her powers, but so it was that nothing which I know of, certainly nothing which the public have seen, was completed in either of those places. I can only state the fact, without assigning any cause for it; but as soon as she was fixed in her second home, she resumed the habits of composition which had been formed in her first, and continued them to the end of her life. The first year of her residence at Chawton seems to have been devoted to revising and preparing for the press *Sense and Sensibility,* and *Pride and Prejudice;* but between February 1811 and August 1816, she began and completed *Mansfield Park, Emma,* and *Persuasion,* so that the last five years of her life produced the same number of novels with those which had been written in her early youth.

Jane Austen lived in entire seclusion from the literary world: neither by correspondence, nor by personal intercourse was she known to any contemporary authors. It is probable that she never was in company with any person whose talents or whose celebrity equalled her own; so that her powers never could have been sharpened by collision with superior intellects, nor her imagination aided by their casual suggestions. Whatever she produced was a genuine home-made article. Even during the last two or three years of her life, when her works were rising in the estimation of the public, they did not enlarge the circle of her acquaintance. Few of her readers knew even her name,[3] and none knew more of her than her name. I doubt whether it would be possible to mention any other author of note, whose personal obscurity was so complete.

Early in the year 1816 some family troubles disturbed the usually tranquil course of Jane Austen's life; and it is probable that the inward malady, which was to prove ultimately fatal,[4] was already felt by her; for some distant friends, whom she visited in the spring of that year, thought that her health was somewhat impaired, and observed that she went about her old haunts, and recalled old recollections connected with them in a particular manner, as if she did not expect ever to see them again. I cannot tell how soon she was aware of the serious nature of her malady. By God's mercy it was not attended with much suffering, but the progress of the disease became more and more manifest as the year advanced. The usual walk was at first shortened, and then discontinued; and air was sought in a donkey-carriage. Gradually, too, her habits of activity within the house ceased, and she was obliged to lie down much. It is certain, however, that the mind did not share in this decay of the bodily strength. *Persuasion* was not finished before the middle of August in that year; and the manner in which it was then completed affords proof that neither the critical nor the creative powers of the author were at all impaired.

Alas! summer [1817] came to her only on her deathbed. March 17th is the last date to be found in the manuscript on which she was engaged; and as the watch of the drowned man indicates the time of his death, so does this final date seem to fix the period when her mind could no longer pursue its accustomed course. Throughout her illness she was nursed by her sister, often assisted by her sister-in-law, my mother. Both were

---

[3] Four of her six great novels were published anonymously during her lifetime. [ED.]

[4] Based on Austen's symptoms as described in some of her letters, at least two modern medical experts have hazarded a tentative diagnosis: one of Addison's disease and another of Hodgkin's disease. [ED.]

with her when she died. Two of her brothers, who were clergy-men, lived near enough to Winchester to be in frequent atten-dance, and to administer the services suitable for a Christian's death-bed. While she used the language of hope to her corre-spondents, she was fully aware of her danger, though not appalled by it. We may well believe that she would gladly have lived longer; but she was enabled without dismay or complaint to prepare for death. When the end at last came, she sank rapidly, and on being asked by her attendants whether there was anything that she wanted, her reply was, "Nothing but death." These were her last words. In quietness and peace she breathed her last on the morning of July 18, 1817.

On the 24th of that month she was buried in Winchester Cathedral, near the centre of the north aisle, almost opposite to the beautiful chantry tomb of William of Wykeham. A large slab of black marble in the pavement marks the place. Her own family only attended the funeral. Her sister returned to her desolated home, there to devote herself, for ten years, to the care of her aged mother; and to live much on the memory of her lost sister, till called many years later to rejoin her. Her brothers went back sorrowing to their homes. They were very fond and very proud of her. They were attached to her by her talents, her virtues, and her engaging manners; and each loved afterwards to fancy a resemblance in some niece or daughter of his own to the dear sister Jane, whose perfect equal they yet never expected to see.

———

Lady Susan is known as one of Jane Austen's epistolary nov-els because the story unfolds entirely through a series of letters exchanged among the main characters. Although the work was thought to be written about 1805 or earlier, it wasn't published until 1871 as an appendix (along with *The Watsons*) to J. E. Austen Leigh's *Memoir*. [ED.]

Lady Susan

LETTER 1

Lady Susan Vernon to Mr. Vernon

Langford, December

My dear Brother

I can no longer refuse myself the pleasure of profiting by your kind invitation, when we last parted, of spending some weeks with you at Churchill, and therefore, if quite convenient to you and Mrs. Vernon to receive me at present, I shall hope within a few days to be introduced to a sister whom I have so long desired to be acquainted with. My kind friends here are most affectionately urgent with me to prolong my stay, but their hospitable and chearful dispositions lead them too much into society for my present situation and state of mind; and I impatiently look forward to the hour when I shall be admitted into your delightful retirement. I long to be made known to your dear little children, in whose hearts I shall be very eager to secure an interest. I shall soon have occasion for all my fortitude, as I am on the point of separation from my own daughter. The long illness of her dear father prevented my paying her that attention which duty and affection equally dictated, and I have too much reason to fear that the governess to whose care I consigned her was unequal to the charge. I have therefore resolved on placing her at one of the best private schools in Town, where I shall have an opportunity of leaving her myself, in my way to you. I am determined, you see, not to be denied admittance at Churchill. It would indeed give me most painful sensations to know that it were not in your power to receive me.

Your most obliged and affectionate sister

S. VERNON

LETTER 2

Lady Susan to Mrs. Johnson

Langford

You were mistaken, my dear Alicia, in supposing me fixed at this place for the rest of the winter. It grieves me to say how greatly you were mistaken, for I have seldom spent three months more agreeably than those which have just flown away. At present, nothing goes smoothly; the females of the family are united against me. You foretold how it would be when I first came to Langford, and Manwaring is so uncommonly pleasing that I was not without apprehensions myself. I remember saying to myself, as I drove to the house, "I like this man; pray heaven no harm come of it!" But I was determined to be discreet, to bear in mind my being only four months a widow, and to be as quiet as possible: and I have been so, my dear creature; I have admitted no one's attentions but Manwaring's. I have avoided all general flirtation whatever; I have distinguished no creature besides, of all the numbers resorting hither, except Sir James Martin, on whom I bestowed a little notice, in order to detach him from Miss Manwaring; but if the world could know my motive *there,* they would honour me. I have been called an unkind mother, but it was the sacred impulse of maternal affection, it was the advantage of my daughter that led me on; and if that daughter were not the greatest simpleton on earth, I might have been rewarded for my exertions as I ought. Sir James did make proposals to me for Frederica—but Frederica, who was born to be the torment of my life, chose to set herself so violently against the match that I thought it better to lay aside the scheme for the present. I have more than once repented that I did not marry him myself; and were he but one degree less contemptibly weak, I certainly should, but I must own myself rather romantic in that respect, and that riches only will not satisfy me. The event of all this is very provoking: Sir James is gone, Maria highly incensed, and Mrs. Manwaring insupportably jealous; so jealous, in short, and so enraged against me, that, in the fury of her temper, I should not be surprised at her appealing to her guardian, if she had the liberty of addressing him—but there your Husband stands my friend; and the kindest, most amiable action of his life was his throwing her off forever on her marriage. Keep up his resentment, therefore, I charge you. We are now in a sad state; no house was ever more altered: the whole family are at war, and Manwaring scarcely dares speak to me. It is time for me to be gone; I have therefore determined on leaving them, and shall spend, I hope, a comfortable day with you in Town within this week. If I am as little in favour with Mr. Johnson as ever, you must come to me at No. 10 Wigmore Street—but I hope this may not be the case, for as Mr. Johnson, with all his faults, is a man to whom that great word "respectable" is always given, and I am known to be so intimate with his wife, his slighting me has an awkward look. I take Town in my way to that insupportable spot, a country village; for I am really going to Churchill. Forgive me, my dear friend, it is my last resource. Were there another place in England open to me, I would prefer it. Charles Vernon is my aversion, and I am afraid of his wife. At Churchill, however, I must remain till I have something better in view. My young lady accompanies me to Town, where I shall deposit her under the care of Miss Summers, in Wigmore Street, till she becomes a little more reasonable. She will make good connections there, as the girls are all of the best families. The price is immense, and much beyond what I can ever attempt to pay.

Adieu. I will send you a line as soon as I arrive in Town. Yours ever,

S. VERNON

LETTER 3

Mrs. Vernon to Lady De Courcy

Churchill

My dear Mother

I am very sorry to tell you that it will not be in our power to keep our promise of spending our Christmas with you; and we are prevented that happiness by a circumstance which is not likely to make us any amends. Lady Susan, in a letter to her brother,

has declared her intention of visiting us almost immediately—
and as such a visit is in all probability merely an affair of convenience, it is impossible to conjecture its length. I was by no
means prepared for such an event, nor can I now account for
her Ladyship's conduct; Langford appeared so exactly the place
for her in every respect, as well from the elegant and expensive
stile of living there, as from her particular attachment to Mrs.
Manwaring, that I was very far from expecting so speedy a dis-
tinction, tho' I always imagined from her increasing friendship
for us since her husband's death, that we should at some future
period be obliged to receive her. Mr. Vernon, I think, was a great
deal too kind to her when he was in Staffordshire; her behaviour
to him, independent of her general character, has been so inex-
cusably artful and ungenerous since our marriage was first in
agitation that no one less amiable and mild than himself could
have overlooked it all; and tho', as his brother's widow, and in
narrow circumstances, it was proper to render her pecuniary
assistance, I cannot help thinking his pressing invitation to her
to visit us at Churchill perfectly unnecessary. Disposed, however, as he always is to think the best of every one, her display of
greif, and professions of regret, and general resolutions of prudence were sufficient to soften his heart, and make him really
confide in her sincerity. But as for myself, I am still uncon-
vinced; and plausibly as her Ladyship has now written, I cannot
make up my mind till I better understand her real meaning in
coming to us. You may guess, therefore, my dear Madam, with
what feelings I look forward to her arrival. She will have occasion for all those attractive powers for which she is celebrated,
to gain any share of my regard; and I shall certainly endeavour
to guard myself against their influence, if not accompanied by
something more substantial. She expresses a most eager desire
of being acquainted with me, and makes very gracious mention
of my children, but I am not quite weak enough to suppose a
woman who has behaved with inattention if not unkindness to
her own child, should be attached to any of mine. Miss Vernon
is to be placed at a school in Town before her mother comes to
us, which I am glad of, for her sake and my own. It must be to
her advantage to be separated from her mother, and a girl of six-

teen who has received so wretched an education could not be a
very desirable companion here. Reginald has long wished, I
know, to see the captivating Lady Susan, and we shall depend on
his joining our party soon. I am glad to hear that my father continues so well; and am, with best love, etc.,

                                              CATH. VERNON

LETTER 4

Mr. De Courcy to Mrs. Vernon

                                              Parklands
My dear Sister
I congratulate you and Mr. Vernon on being about to receive
into your family the most accomplished coquette in England. As
a very distinguished flirt, I have always been taught to consider
her; but it has lately fallen in my way to hear some particulars of
her conduct at Langford, which proves that she does not confine
herself to that sort of honest flirtation which satisfies most
people, but aspires to the more delicious gratification of making
a whole family miserable. By her behaviour to Mr. Manwaring
she gave jealousy and wretchedness to his wife, and by her
attentions to a young man previously attached to Mr. Manwaring's
sister deprived an amiable girl of her lover. I learnt all this from
a Mr. Smith, now in this neighbourhood—(I have dined with
him, at Hurst and Wilford)—who is just come from Langford,
where he was a fortnight in the house with her Ladyship, and
who is therefore well qualified to make the communication.

What a woman she must be! I long to see her, and shall certainly accept your kind invitation, that I may form some idea of
those bewitching powers which can do so much—engaging at
the same time, and in the same house, the affections of two
men, who were neither of them at liberty to bestow them—and
all this without the charm of youth. I am glad to find Miss
Vernon does not accompany her mother to Churchill, as she has
not even manners to recommend her, and according to Mr.
Smith's account, is equally dull and proud. Where pride and stu-
pidity unite there can be no dissimulation worthy notice, and

Miss Vernon shall be consigned to unrelenting contempt; but by all that I can gather, Lady Susan possesses a degree of captivating deceit which it must be pleasing to witness and detect. I shall be with you very soon, and am

your affectionate brother R. DE COURCY

LETTER 5

Lady Susan to Mrs. Johnson

Churchill

I received your note, my dear Alicia, just before I left Town, and rejoice to be assured that Mr. Johnson suspected nothing of your engagement the evening before. It is undoubtedly better to deceive him entirely; since he will be stubborn, he must be tricked. I arrived here in safety, and have no reason to complain of my reception from Mr. Vernon; but I confess myself not equally satisfied with the behaviour of his lady. She is perfectly well-bred, indeed, and has the air of a woman of fashion, but her manners are not such as can persuade me of her being prepossessed in my favour. I wanted her to be delighted at seeing me— I was as amiable as possible on the occasion—but all in vain— she does not like me. To be sure, when we consider that I *did* take some pains to prevent my brother-in-law's marrying her, this want of cordiality is not very surprising—and yet it shews an illiberal and vindictive spirit to resent a project which influenced me six years ago, and which never succeeded at last. I am sometimes half disposed to repent that I did not let Charles buy Vernon Castle, when we were obliged to sell it; but it was a trying circumstance, especially as the sale took place exactly at the time of his marriage—and everybody ought to respect the delicacy of those feelings which could not endure that my husband's dignity should be lessened by his younger brother's having possession of the family estate. Could matters have been so arranged as to prevent the necessity of our leaving the Castle, could we have lived with Charles and kept him single, I should have been very far from persuading my husband to dispose of it elsewhere; but Charles was then on the point of marrying Miss De Courcy, and the event has justified me. Here are children in abundance, and what benefit could have accrued to me from his purchasing Vernon? My having prevented it may perhaps have given his wife an unfavourable impression—but where there is a disposition to dislike, a motive will never be wanting; and as to money-matters it has not withheld him from being very useful to me. I really have a regard for him, he is so easily imposed on!

The house is a good one, the furniture fashionable, and everything announces plenty and elegance. Charles is very rich, I am sure; when a man has once got his name in a Banking House, he rolls in money. But they do not know what to do with it, keep very little company, and never go to Town but on business. We shall be as stupid as possible. I mean to win my sister-in-law's heart through the children; I know all their names already, and am going to attach myself with the greatest sensibility to one in particular, a young Frederic, whom I take on my lap and sigh over for his dear uncle's sake.

Poor Manwaring!—I need not tell you how much I miss him—how perpetually he is in my thoughts. I found a dismal letter from him on my arrival here, full of complaints of his wife and sister, and lamentations on the cruelty of his fate. I passed off the letter as his wife's, to the Vernons, and when I write to him, it must be under cover to you.

Yours ever, S. V.

LETTER 6

Mrs. Vernon to Mr. De Courcy

Churchill

Well, my dear Reginald, I have seen this dangerous creature, and must give you some description of her, tho' I hope you will soon be able to form your own judgement. She is really excessively pretty. However you may chuse to question the allurements of a lady no longer young, I must, for my own part, declare that I have seldom seen so lovely a woman as Lady

Susan. She is delicately fair, with fine grey eyes and dark eye-lashes; and from her appearance one would not suppose her more than five and twenty, tho' she must in fact be ten years older. I was certainly not disposed to admire her, tho' always hearing she was beautiful; but I cannot help feeling that she possesses an uncommon union of symmetry, brilliancy, and grace. Her address to me was so gentle, frank, and even affectionate, that, if I had not known how much she has always disliked me for marrying Mr. Vernon, and that we had never met before, I should have imagined her an attached friend. One is apt, I beleive, to connect assurance of manner with coquetry, and to expect that an impudent address will naturally attend an impudent mind; at least I was myself prepared for an improper degree of confidence in Lady Susan; but her countenance is absolutely sweet, and her voice and manner winningly mild. I am sorry it is so, for what is this but deceit? Unfortunately, one knows her too well. She is clever and agreable, has all that knowledge of the world which makes conversation easy, and talks very well with a happy command of language, which is too often used, I beleive, to make black appear white. She has already almost persuaded me of her being warmly attached to her daughter, tho' I have been so long convinced to the contrary. She speaks of her with so much tenderness and anxiety, lamenting so bitterly the neglect of her education, which she represents however as wholly unavoidable, that I am forced to recollect how many successive springs her Ladyship spent in Town, while her daughter was left in Staffordshire to the care of servants, or a governess very little better, to prevent my beleiving what she says.

If her manners have so great an influence on my resentful heart, you may judge how much more strongly they operate on Mr. Vernon's generous temper. I wish I could be as well satisfied as he is, that it was really her choice to leave Langford for Churchill; and if she had not staid three months there before she discovered that her friends' manner of living did not suit her situation or feelings, I might have beleived that concern for the loss of such a husband as Mr. Vernon, to whom her own behaviour was far from unexceptionable, might for a time make her wish for retirement. But I cannot forget the length of her visit to the Manwarings; and when I reflect on the different mode of life which she led with them, from that to which she must now submit, I can only suppose that the wish of establishing her reputation by following, tho' late, the path of propriety, occasioned her removal from a family where she must in reality have been particularly happy. Your friend Mr. Smith's story, however, cannot be quite true, as she corresponds regularly with Mrs. Manwaring. At any rate it must be exaggerated; it is scarcely possible that two men should be so grossly deceived by her at once.

Yours etc. CATH. VERNON

LETTER 7

Lady Susan to Mrs. Johnson

Churchill

My dear Alicia

You are very good in taking notice of Frederica, and I am grateful for it as a mark of your friendship; but as I cannot have any doubt of the warmth of that friendship, I am far from exacting so heavy a sacrifice. She is a stupid girl, and has nothing to recommend her. I would not, therefore, on any account have you encumber one moment of your precious time by sending her to Edward Street, especially as every visit is so many hours deducted from the grand affair of education, which I really wish to be attended to while she remains with Miss Summers. I want her to play and sing with some portion of taste and a good deal of assurance, as she has *my* hand and arm, and a tolerable voice. *I* was so much indulged in my infant years that I was never obliged to attend to anything, and consequently am without the accomplishments which are now necessary to finish a pretty woman. Not that I am an advocate for the prevailing fashion of acquiring a perfect knowledge of all languages, arts, and sciences. It is throwing time away; to be mistress of

French, Italian, and German, Music, Singing, Drawing, etc. will gain a woman some applause, but will not add one lover to her list. Grace and manner, after all, are of the greatest importance. I do not mean, therefore, that Frederica's acquirements should be more than superficial, and I flatter myself that she will not remain long enough at school to understand anything thoroughly. I hope to see her the wife of Sir James within a twelvemonth. You know on what I ground my hope, and it is certainly a good foundation, for school must be very humiliating to a girl of Frederica's age. And by the by, you had better not invite her any more on that account, as I wish her to find her situation as unpleasant as possible. I am sure of Sir James at any time, and could make him renew his application by a line. I shall trouble you meanwhile to prevent his forming any other attachment when he comes to Town. Ask him to your house occasionally, and talk to him of Frederica, that he may not forget her.

Upon the whole, I commend my own conduct in this affair extremely, and regard it as a very happy instance of circumspection and tenderness. Some mothers would have insisted on their daughter's accepting so good an offer on the first overture, but I could not answer it to myself to force Frederica into a marriage from which her heart revolted; and instead of adopting so harsh a measure, merely propose to make it her own choice, by rendering her thoroughly uncomfortable till she does accept him. But enough of this tiresome girl.

You may well wonder how I contrive to pass my time here—and for the first week it was most insufferably dull. Now, however, we begin to mend; our party is enlarged by Mrs. Vernon's brother, a handsome young man, who promises me some amusement. There is something about him which rather interests me, a sort of sauciness and familiarity which I shall teach him to correct. He is lively and seems clever, and when I have inspired him with greater respect for me than his sister's kind offices have implanted, he may be an agreable flirt. There is exquisite pleasure in subduing an insolent spirit, in making a person predetermined to dislike, acknowledge one's superiority.

I have disconcerted him already by my calm reserve, and it shall be my endeavour to humble the pride of these self-important De Courcys still lower, to convince Mrs. Vernon that her sisterly cautions have been bestowed in vain, and to persuade Reginald that she has scandalously belied me. This project will serve at least to amuse me, and prevent my feeling so acutely this dreadful separation from you and all whom I love. Adieu.

Yours ever
S. VERNON

LETTER 8

Mrs. Vernon to Lady De Courcy

Churchill

My dear Mother

You must not expect Reginald back again for some time. He desires me to tell you that the present open weather induced him to accept Mr. Vernon's invitation to prolong his stay in Sussex, that they may have some hunting together. He means to send for his horses immediately, and it is impossible to say when you may see him in Kent. I will not disguise my sentiments on this change from you, my dear Madam, tho' I think you had better not communicate them to my father, whose excessive anxiety about Reginald would subject him to an alarm which might seriously affect his health and spirits. Lady Susan has certainly contrived, in the space of a fortnight, to make my brother like her. In short, I am persuaded that his continuing here beyond the time originally fixed for his return is occasioned as much by a degree of fascination towards her, as by the wish of hunting with Mr. Vernon, and of course I cannot receive that pleasure from the length of his visit which my brother's company would otherwise give me. I am, indeed, provoked at the artifice of this unprincipled woman. What stronger proof of her dangerous abilities can be given than this perversion of Reginald's judgement, which when he entered the house was so decidedly against her? In his last letter he actually gave me some particulars of her behaviour at Langford, such as he received from a gentleman who knew her perfectly well, which, if true, must raise abhorrence against her, and which Reginald himself was entirely disposed to credit. His opinion of her, I am sure, was as low as of any woman in England; and when he first came it was evident that he considered her as one entitled neither to delicacy nor respect, and that he felt she would be delighted with the attentions of any man inclined to flirt with her.

Her behaviour, I confess, has been calculated to do away with such an idea; I have not detected the smallest impropriety in it, nothing of vanity, of pretension, of levity—and she is altogether so attractive that I should not wonder at his being delighted with her, had he known nothing of her previous to this personal acquaintance; but against reason, against conviction, to be so well pleased with her, as I am sure he is, does really astonish me. His admiration was at first very strong, but no more than was natural, and I did not wonder at his being much struck by the gentleness and delicacy of her manners; but when he has mentioned her of late it has been in terms of more extraordinary praise; and yesterday he actually said that he could not be surprised at any effect produced on the heart of man by such loveliness and such abilities; and when I lamented, in reply, the badness of her disposition, he observed that whatever might have been her errors, they were to be imputed to her neglected education and early marriage, and that she was altogether a wonderful woman.

This tendency to excuse her conduct, or to forget it in the warmth of admiration, vexes me; and if I did not know that Reginald is too much at home at Churchill to need an invitation for lengthening his visit, I should regret Mr. Vernon's giving him any.

Lady Susan's intentions are of course those of absolute coquetry, or a desire of universal admiration. I cannot for a moment imagine that she has anything more serious in view; but it mortifies me to see a young man of Reginald's sense duped by her at all. I am, etc.

CATH. VERNON

LETTER 9

Mrs. Johnson to Lady Susan

Edward St.

My dearest Friend

I congratulate you on Mr. De Courcy's arrival, and I advise you by all means to marry him; his father's Estate is, we know, considerable, and I beleive certainly entailed. Sir Reginald is very infirm, and not likely to stand in your way long. I hear the young man well spoken of; and tho' no one can really deserve you, my dearest Susan, Mr. De Courcy may be worth having. Manwaring will storm of course, but you may easily pacify him. Besides, the most scrupulous point of honour could not require you to wait for *his* emancipation. I have seen Sir James; he came to Town for a few days last week, and called several times in Edward Street. I talked to him about you and your daughter, and he is so far from having forgotten you, that I am sure he would marry either of you with pleasure. I gave him hopes of Frederica's relenting, and told him a great deal of her improvements. I scolded him for making love to Maria Manwaring; he protested that he had been only in joke, and we both laughed heartily at her disappointment; and, in short, were very agreable. He is as silly as ever. Yours faithfully

ALICIA

LETTER 10

Lady Susan Vernon to Mrs. Johnson

Churchill

I am obliged to you, my dear friend, for your advice respecting Mr. De Courcy, which I know was given with the full conviction of its expediency, tho' I am not quite determined on following it. I cannot easily resolve on anything so serious as marriage; especially as I am not at present in want of money, and might perhaps, till the old gentleman's death, be very little benefited by the match. It is true that I am vain enough to beleive it within my reach. I have made him sensible of my power, and can now enjoy the pleasure of triumphing over a mind prepared to dislike me, and prejudiced against all my past actions. His sister, too, is, I hope, convinced how little the ungenerous representations of any one to the disadvantage of another will avail when opposed to the immediate influence of intellect and manner. I see plainly that she is uneasy at my progress in the good opinion of her brother, and conclude that nothing will be wanting on her part to counteract me; but having once made him doubt the justice of her opinion of me, I think I may defy her.

It has been delightful to me to watch his advances towards intimacy, especially to observe his altered manner in consequence of my repressing by the calm dignity of my deportment his insolent approach to direct familiarity. My conduct has been equally guarded from the first, and I never behaved less like a coquette in the whole course of my life, tho' perhaps my desire of dominion was never more decided. I have subdued him entirely by sentiment and serious conversation, and made him, I may venture to say, at least *half* in love with me, without the semblance of the most commonplace flirtation. Mrs. Vernon's consciousness of deserving every sort of revenge that it can be in my power to inflict for her ill-offices could alone enable her to perceive that I am actuated by any design in behaviour so gentle and unpretending. Let her think and act as she chuses, however. I have never yet found that the advice of a Sister could prevent a young Man's being in love if he chose it. We are advancing now towards some kind of confidence, and in short are likely to be engaged in a sort of platonic friendship. On *my* side you may be sure of its never being more, for if I were not already as much attached to another person as I can be to any one, I should make a point of not bestowing my affection on a man who had dared to think so meanly of me.

Reginald has a good figure, and is not unworthy the praise you have heard given him, but is still greatly inferior to our friend at Langford. He is less polished, less insinuating than Manwaring, and is comparatively deficient in the power of saying those delightful things which put one in good humour with oneself and all the world. He is quite agreeable enough, however, to afford me amusement, and to make many of those hours pass very pleasantly which would otherwise be spent in endeavouring to overcome my sister-in-law's reserve, and listening to her husband's insipid talk.

Your account of Sir James is most satisfactory, and I mean to give Miss Frederica a hint of my intentions very soon. Yours, etc.

S. VERNON

LETTER 11

Mrs. Vernon to Lady De Courcy
Churchill

I really grow quite uneasy, my dearest mother, about Reginald, from witnessing the very rapid increase of Lady Susan's influence. They are now on terms of the most particular friendship, frequently engaged in long conversations together; and she has contrived by the most artful coquetry to subdue his judgement to her own purposes. It is impossible to see the intimacy between them so very soon established without some alarm, tho' I can hardly suppose that Lady Susan's views extend to marriage. I wish you could get Reginald home again under any plausible pretence; he is not at all disposed to leave us, and I have given him as many hints of my father's precarious state of health as common decency will allow me to do in my own house. Her power over him must now be boundless, as she has entirely effaced all his former ill-opinion, and persuaded him not merely to forget but to justify her conduct. Mr. Smith's account of her proceedings at Langford, where he accused her of having made Mr. Manwaring and a young man engaged to Miss Manwaring distractedly in love with her, which Reginald firmly beleived when he came to Churchill, is now, he is persuaded, only a scandalous invention. He has told me so in a warmth of manner which spoke his regret at having ever beleived the contrary himself.

How sincerely do I grieve that she ever entered this house! I always looked forward to her coming with uneasiness—but very far was it from originating in anxiety for Reginald. I expected a most disagreable companion for myself, but could not imagine that my brother would be in the smallest danger of being captivated by a woman with whose principles he was so well acquainted, and whose character he so heartily despised. If you can get him away, it will be a good thing.

Yours affectionately

CATH. VERNON

LETTER 12

Sir Reginald De Courcy to his Son

Parklands

I know that young men in general do not admit of any inquiry even from their nearest relations into affairs of the heart, but I hope, my dear Reginald, that you will be superior to such as allow nothing for a father's anxiety, and think themselves privileged to refuse him their confidence and slight his advice. You must be sensible that as an only son, and the representative of an ancient family, your conduct in life is most interesting to your connections. In the very important concern of marriage especially, there is everything at stake—your own happiness, that of your parents, and the credit of your name. I do not suppose that you would deliberately form an absolute engagement of that nature without acquainting your mother and myself, or at least without being convinced that we should approve of your choice; but I cannot help fearing that you may be drawn in, by the lady who has lately attached you, to a marriage which the whole of your family, far and near, must highly reprobate.

Lady Susan's age is itself a material objection, but her want of character is one so much more serious that the difference of even twelve years becomes in comparison of small account. Were you not blinded by a sort of fascination, it would be ridiculous in me to repeat the instances of great misconduct on her side, so very generally known. Her neglect of her husband, her encouragement of other men, her extravagance and dissipation, were so gross and notorious that no one could be ignorant of them at the time, nor can now have forgotten them. To our family she has always been represented in softened colours by the benevolence of Mr. Charles Vernon; and yet, in spite of his generous endeavours to excuse her, we know that she did, from the most selfish motives, take all possible pains to prevent his marrying Catherine.

My years and increasing infirmities make me very desirous, my dear Reginald, of seeing you settled in the world. To the fortune of your wife, the goodness of my own will make me indifferent; but her family and character must be equally unexceptionable. When your choice is so fixed as that no objection can be made to either, I can promise you a ready and chearful consent; but it is my duty to oppose a match which deep art only could render probable, and must in the end make wretched.

It is possible her behaviour may arise only from vanity, or the wish of gaining the admiration of a man whom she must imagine to be particularly prejudiced against her; but it is more likely that she should aim at something farther. She is poor, and may naturally seek an alliance which may be advantageous to herself. You know your own rights, and that it is out of my power to prevent your inheriting the family estate. My ability of distressing you during my life would be a species of revenge to which I should hardly stoop under any circumstances. I honestly tell you my sentiments and intentions: I do not wish to work on your fears, but on your sense and affection. It would destroy every comfort of my life to know that you were married to Lady Susan Vernon: it would be the death of that honest pride with which I have hitherto considered my son; I should blush to see him, to hear of him, to think of him.

I may perhaps do no good but that of relieving my own mind by this letter, but I felt it my duty to tell you that your partiality for Lady Susan is no secret to your friends, and to warn you against her. I should be glad to hear your reasons for disbeleiving Mr. Smith's intelligence; you had no doubt of its authenticity a month ago.

If you can give me your assurance of having no design beyond enjoying the conversation of a clever woman for a short period, and of yielding admiration only to her beauty and abilities, without being blinded by them to her faults, you will restore me to happiness; but if you cannot do this, explain to me, at least, what has occasioned so great an alteration in your opinion of her.

I am, etc.

REGINALD DE COURCY

LETTER 13

Lady De Courcy to Mrs. Vernon

Parklands

My dear Catherine

Unluckily I was confined to my room when your last letter came, by a cold which affected my eyes so much as to prevent my reading it myself; so I could not refuse your father when he offered to read it to me, by which means he became acquainted, to my great vexation, with all your fears about your brother. I had intended to write to Reginald myself as soon as my eyes would let me, to point out as well as I could the danger of an intimate acquaintance with so artful a woman as Lady Susan, to a young man of his age and high expectations. I meant, moreover, to have reminded him of our being quite alone now, and very much in need of him to keep up our spirits these long winter evenings. Whether it would have done any good can never be settled now, but I am excessively vexed that Sir Reginald should know anything of a matter which we foresaw would make him so uneasy. He caught all your fears the moment he had read your letter, and I am sure has not had the business out of his head since. He wrote by the same post to Reginald a long letter full of it all, and particularly asking an explanation of what he may have heard from Lady Susan to contradict the late shocking reports. His answer came this morning, which I shall enclose to you, as I think you will like to see it. I wish it was more satisfactory; but it seems written with such a determination to think well of Lady Susan, that his assurances as to marriage, etc., do not set my heart at ease. I say all I can, however, to satisfy your

father, and he is certainly less uneasy since Reginald's letter.
How provoking it is, my dear Catherine, that this unwelcome
guest of yours should not only prevent our meeting this
Christmas, but be the occasion of so much vexation and trouble.
Kiss the dear children for me. Your affectionate mother.

C. DE COURCY

LETTER 14

Mr. De Courcy to Sir Reginald

Churchill

My dear Sir

I have this moment received your letter, which has given me
more astonishment than I ever felt before. I am to thank my sister, I suppose, for having represented me in such a light as to
injure me in your opinion, and give you all this alarm. I know not
why she should chuse to make herself and her family uneasy by
apprehending an event which no one but herself, I can affirm,
would ever have thought possible. To impute such a design to
Lady Susan would be taking from her every claim to that excellent understanding which her bitterest enemies have never
denied her; and equally low must sink my pretensions to common sense if I am suspected of matrimonial views in my behaviour to her. Our difference of age must be an insuperable objection, and I entreat you, my dear sir, to quiet your mind, and no
longer harbour a suspicion which cannot be more injurious to
your own peace than to our understandings.

I can have no other view in remaining with Lady Susan than
to enjoy for a short time (as you have yourself expressed it) the
conversation of a woman of high mental powers. If Mrs. Vernon
would allow something to my affection for herself and her husband in the length of my visit, she would do more justice to us
all; but my sister is unhappily prejudiced beyond the hope of
conviction against Lady Susan. From an attachment to her husband, which in itself does honour to both, she cannot forgive the
endeavours at preventing their union which have been attrib-
uted to selfishness in Lady Susan; but in this case, as well as in

many others, the world has most grossly injured that lady, by supposing the worst where the motives of her conduct have been doubtful.

Lady Susan had heard something so materially to the disadvantage of my sister, as to persuade her that the happiness of Mr. Vernon, to whom she was always much attached, would be absolutely destroyed by the marriage. And this circumstance, while it explains the true motive of Lady Susan's conduct, and removes all the blame which has been so lavished on her, may also convince us how little the general report of any one ought to be credited; since no character, however upright, can escape the malevolence of slander. If my sister, in the security of retirement, with as little opportunity as inclination to do evil, could not avoid censure, we must not rashly condemn those who, living in the world and surrounded with temptation, should be accused of errors which they are known to have the power of committing.

I blame myself severely for having so easily beleived the scandalous tales invented by Charles Smith to the prejudice of Lady Susan, as I am now convinced how greatly they have traduced her. As to Mrs. Manwaring's jealousy, it was totally his own invention, and his account of her attaching Miss Manwaring's lover was scarcely better founded. Sir James Martin had been drawn in by that young lady to pay her some attention; and as he is a man of fortune, it was easy to see that *her* views extended to marriage. It is well known that Miss Manwaring is absolutely on the catch for a husband, and no one therefore can pity her for losing, by the superior attractions of another woman, the chance of being able to make a worthy man completely miserable. Lady Susan was far from intending such a conquest, and on finding how warmly Miss Manwaring resented her lover's defection, determined, in spite of Mr. and Mrs. Manwaring's most earnest entreaties, to leave the family. I have reason to imagine that she did receive serious proposals from Sir James, but her removing to Langford immediately on the discovery of his attachment, must acquit her on that article with every mind of common candour. You will, I am sure, my dear Sir, feel the truth of this, and will hereby learn to do justice to the character of a very injured woman.

I know that Lady Susan in coming to Churchill was governed only by the most honourable and amiable intentions; her prudence and economy are exemplary, her regard for Mr. Vernon equal even to *his* deserts; and her wish of obtaining my sister's good opinion merits a better return than it has received. As a mother she is unexceptionable; her solid affection for her child is shewn by placing her in hands where her education will be properly attended to; but because she has not the blind and weak partiality of most mothers, she is accused of wanting maternal tenderness. Every person of sense, however, will know how to value and commend her well-directed affection, and will join me in wishing that Frederica Vernon may prove more worthy than she has yet done of her mother's tender care.

I have now, my dear Sir, written my real sentiments of Lady Susan; you will know from this letter how highly I admire her abilities, and esteem her character; but if you are not equally convinced by my full and solemn assurance that your fears have been most idly created, you will deeply mortify and distress me. I am, etc.

R. DE COURCY

LETTER 15

Mrs. Vernon to Lady De Courcy
                                                     Churchill
My dear Mother
I return you Reginald's letter, and rejoice with all my heart that my father is made easy by it. Tell him so, with my congratulations; but between ourselves, I must own it has only convinced *me* of my brother's having no *present* intention of marrying Lady Susan—not that he is in no danger of doing so three months hence. He gives a very plausible account of her behaviour at Langford; I wish it may be true, but his intelligence must come from herself, and I am less disposed to beleive it than to lament

the degree of intimacy subsisting between them implied by the discussion of such a subject.

I am sorry to have incurred his displeasure, but can expect nothing better while he is so very eager in Lady Susan's justification. He is very severe against me indeed, and yet I hope I have not been hasty in my judgement of her. Poor woman! tho' I have reasons enough for my dislike, I cannot help pitying her at present, as she is in real distress, and with too much cause. She had this morning a letter from the lady with whom she has placed her daughter, to request that Miss Vernon might be immediately removed, as she had been detected in an attempt to run away. Why, or whither she intended to go, does not appear; but as her situation seems to have been unexceptionable, it is a sad thing, and of course highly afflicting to Lady Susan.

Frederica must be as much as sixteen, and ought to know better; but from what her mother insinuates, I am afraid she is a perverse girl. She has been sadly neglected, however, and her mother ought to remember it.

Mr. Vernon set off for Town as soon as she had determined what should be done. He is, if possible, to prevail on Miss Summers to let Frederica continue with her; and if he cannot succeed, to bring her to Churchill for the present, till some other situation can be found for her. Her Ladyship is comforting herself meanwhile by strolling along the shrubbery with Reginald, calling forth all his tender feelings, I suppose, on this distressing occasion. She has been talking a great deal about it to me. She talks vastly well; I am afraid of being ungenerous, or I should say *too* well to feel so very deeply. But I will not look for faults; she may be Reginald's wife. Heaven forbid it! but why should I be quicker-sighted than anybody else? Mr. Vernon declares that he never saw deeper distress than hers, on the receipt of the letter—and is his judgement inferior to mine?

She was very unwilling that Frederica should be allowed to come to Churchill, and justly enough, as it seems a sort of reward to behaviour deserving very differently; but it was impossible to take her anywhere else, and she is not to remain here long.

"It will be absolutely necessary, said she, as you, my dear

sister, must be sensible, to treat my daughter with some severity while she is here; a most painful necessity, but I will endeavour to submit to it. I am afraid I have often been too indulgent, but my poor Frederica's temper could never bear opposition well. You must support and encourage me—You must urge the necessity of reproof if you see me too lenient."

All this sounds very reasonably. Reginald is so incensed against the poor silly girl! Surely it is not to Lady Susan's credit that he should be so bitter against her daughter; his idea of her must be drawn from the mother's description.

Well, whatever may be his fate, we have the comfort of knowing that we have done our utmost to save him. We must commit the event to an Higher Power. Yours ever etc.

CATH. VERNON

LETTER 16

Lady Susan to Mrs. Johnson

Churchill

Never, my dearest Alicia, was I so provoked in my life as by a letter this morning from Miss Summers. That horrid girl of mine has been trying to run away. I had not a notion of her being such a little devil before, she seemed to have all the Vernon milkiness; but on receiving the letter in which I declared my intention about Sir James, she actually attempted to elope; at least, I cannot otherwise account for her doing it. She meant, I suppose, to go to the Clarkes in Staffordshire, for she has no other acquaintance. But she *shall* be punished, she *shall* have him. I have sent Charles to Town to make matters up if he can, for I do not by any means want her here. If Miss Summers will not keep her, you must find me out another school, unless we can get her married immediately. Miss S. writes word that she could not get the young lady to assign any cause for her extraordinary conduct, which confirms me in my own private explanation of it.

Frederica is too shy, I think, and too much in awe of me to tell tales; but if the mildness of her uncle *should* get anything from her, I am not afraid. I trust I shall be able to make my story as good as hers. If I am vain of anything, it is of my eloquence. Consideration and esteem as surely follow command of language, as admiration waits on beauty. And here I have opportunity enough for the exercise of my talent, as the cheif of my time is spent in conversation. Reginald is never easy unless we are by ourselves, and when the weather is tolerable, we pace the shrubbery for hours together. I like him on the whole very well; he is clever and has a good deal to say, but he is sometimes impertinent and troublesome. There is a sort of ridiculous delicacy about him which requires the fullest explanation of whatever he may have heard to my disadvantage, and is never satisfied till he thinks he has ascertained the beginning and end of everything.

This is *one* sort of love—but I confess it does not particularly recommend itself to me. I infinitely prefer the tender and liberal spirit of Manwaring, which, impressed with the deepest conviction of my merit, is satisfied that whatever I do must be right; and look with a degree of contempt on the inquisitive and doubtful fancies of that heart which seems always debating on the reasonableness of its emotions. Manwaring is indeed beyond compare, superior to Reginald—superior in everything but the power of being with me. Poor fellow! he is quite distracted by jealousy, which I am not sorry for, as I know no better support of love. He has been teizing me to allow of his coming into this country, and lodging somewhere near me *incog.*—but I forbid anything of the kind. Those women are inexcusable who forget what is due to themselves and the opinion of the world.

S. VERNON.

LETTER 17

Mrs. Vernon to Lady De Courcy

Churchill

My dear Mother

Mr. Vernon returned on Thursday night, bringing his neice with him. Lady Susan had received a line from him by that day's post, informing her that Miss Summers had absolutely refused to allow of Miss Vernon's continuance in her academy; we were therefore prepared for her arrival, and expected them impatiently the whole evening. They came while we were at tea, and I never saw any creature look so frightened in my life as Frederica when she entered the room.

Lady Susan, who had been shedding tears before, and shewing great agitation at the idea of the meeting, received her with perfect self-command, and without betraying the least tenderness of spirit. She hardly spoke to her, and on Frederica's bursting into tears as soon [as] we were seated, took her out of the room, and did not return for some time. When she did, her eyes looked very red, and she was as much agitated as before. We saw no more of her daughter.

Poor Reginald was beyond measure concerned to see his fair friend in such distress, and watched her with so much tender solicitude that I, who occasionally caught her observing his countenance with exultation, was quite out of patience. This pathetic representation lasted the whole evening, and so ostentatious and artful a display had entirely convinced me that she did in fact feel nothing.

I am more angry with her than ever since I have seen her daughter; the poor girl looks so unhappy that my heart aches for her. Lady Susan is surely too severe, for Frederica does not seem to have the sort of temper to make severity necessary. She looks perfectly timid, dejected, and penitent.

She is very pretty, tho' not so handsome as her mother, nor at all like her. Her complexion is delicate, but neither so fair nor so blooming as Lady Susan's—and she has quite the Vernon cast of countenance, the oval face and mild dark eyes, and there is peculiar sweetness in her look when she speaks either to her uncle or me, for as we behave kindly to her we have of course engaged her gratitude. Her mother has insinuated that her temper is untractable, but I never saw a face less indicative of any evil disposition than hers; and from what I now see of the behaviour of each to the other, the invariable severity of Lady Susan and the silent dejection of Frederica, I am led to beleive as heretofore that the former has no real love for her daughter, and has never done her justice or treated her affectionately.

I have not yet been able to have any conversation with my neice; she is shy, and I think I can see that some pains are taken to prevent her being much with me. Nothing satisfactory transpires as to her reason for running away. Her kind-hearted uncle, you may be sure, was too fearful of distressing her to ask many questions as they travelled. I wish it had been possible for me to fetch her instead of him; I think I should have discovered the truth in the course of a thirty-mile journey.

The small pianoforté has been removed within these few days, at Lady Susan's request, into her dressing room, and Frederica spends great part of the day there; *practising*, it is called; but I seldom hear any noise when I pass that way. What she does with herself there, I do not know; there are plenty of books in the room, but it is not every girl who has been running wild the first fifteen years of her life, that can or will read. Poor creature! the prospect from her window is not very instructive, for that room overlooks the lawn, you know, with the shrubbery on one side, where she may see her mother walking for an hour together in earnest conversation with Reginald. A girl of Frederica's age must be childish indeed, if such things do not strike her. Is it not inexcusable to give such an example to a daughter? Yet Reginald still thinks Lady Susan the best of mothers—still condemns Frederica as a worthless girl! He is convinced that her attempt to run away proceeded from no justifiable cause, and had no provocation. I am sure I cannot say that it *had*, but while Miss Summers declares that Miss Vernon shewed no signs of obstinacy or perverseness during her whole stay in Wigmore Street till she was detected in this scheme, I cannot so readily credit what Lady Susan has made him and wants to make me beleive, that it was merely an impatience of restraint and a desire of escaping from the tuition of masters which brought on the plan of an elopement. Oh! Reginald, how is your judgement enslaved! He scarcely dares even allow her to be handsome, and when I speak of her beauty, replies only that her eyes have no brilliancy.

Sometimes he is sure she is deficient in understanding, and at others that her temper only is in fault. In short, when a person is always to deceive, it is impossible to be consistent. Lady Susan finds it necessary for her own justification that Frederica should be to blame, and probably has sometimes judged it expedient to accuse her of ill-nature and sometimes to lament her want of sense. Reginald is only repeating after her Ladyship.

I am etc.

CATH. VERNON

LETTER 18

From the same to the same

Churchill

My dear Madam

I am very glad to find that my description of Frederica Vernon has interested you, for I do beleive her truly deserving of your regard; and when I have communicated a notion which has recently struck me, your kind impressions in her favour will, I am sure, be heightened. I cannot help fancying that she is growing partial to my brother; I so very often see her eyes fixed on his face with a remarkable expression of pensive admiration! He is certainly very handsome—and yet more—there is an openness in his manner that must be highly prepossessing, and I am sure she feels it so. Thoughtful and pensive in general, her countenance always brightens into a smile when Reginald says anything amusing; and, let the subject be ever so serious that he may be conversing on, I am much mistaken if a syllable of his uttering escapes her.

I want to make *him* sensible of all this, for we know the power of gratitude on such a heart as his; and could Frederica's artless affection detach him from her mother, we might bless the day which brought her to Churchill. I think, my dear Madam, you would not disapprove of her as a daughter. She is extremely young, to be sure, has had a wretched education, and a dreadful example of levity in her mother; but yet I can pronounce her disposition to be excellent, and her natural abilities very good.

Tho' totally without accomplishments, she is by no means so ignorant as one might expect to find her, being fond of books and spending the cheif of her time in reading. Her mother leaves her more to herself now than she *did,* and I have her with me as much as possible, and have taken great pains to overcome her timidity. We are very good friends, and tho' she never opens her lips before her mother, she talks enough when alone with me to make it clear that, if properly treated by Lady Susan, she would always appear to much greater advantage. There cannot be a more gentle, affectionate heart; or more obliging manners, when acting without restraint. Her little cousins are all very fond of her.

Yours affectionately
CATH. VERNON

LETTER 19

Lady Susan to Mrs. Johnson

Churchill

You will be eager, I know, to hear something farther of Frederica, and perhaps may think me negligent for not writing before. She arrived with her uncle last Thursday fortnight, when, of course, I lost no time in demanding the reason of her behaviour; and soon found myself to have been perfectly right in attributing it to my own letter. The purport of it frightened her so thoroughly that, with a mixture of true girlish perverseness and folly, without considering that she could not escape from my authority by running away from Wigmore Street, she resolved on getting out of the house and proceeding directly by the stage to her friends, the Clarkes; and had really got as far as the length of two streets in her journey when she was fortunately missed, pursued, and overtaken.

Such was the first distinguished exploit of Miss Frederica Susanna Vernon; and if we consider that it was achieved at the tender age of sixteen, we shall have room for the most flattering prognostics of her future renown. I am excessively provoked, however, at the parade of propriety which prevented Miss

Summers from keeping the girl; and it seems so extraordinary a piece of nicety, considering my daughter's family connections, that I can only suppose the lady to be governed by the fear of never getting her money. Be that as it may, however, Frederica is returned on my hands; and having now nothing else to employ her, is busy in pursuing the plan of romance begun at Langford. She is actually falling in love with Reginald De Courcy. To disobey her mother by refusing an unexceptionable offer is not enough; her affections must likewise be given without her mother's approbation. I never saw a girl of her age bid fairer to be the sport of mankind. Her feelings are tolerably lively, and she is so charmingly artless in their display as to afford the most reasonable hope of her being ridiculed and despised by every man who sees her.

Artlessness will never do in love matters; and that girl is born a simpleton who has it either by nature or affectation. I am not yet certain that Reginald sees what she is about; nor is it of much consequence. She is now an object of indifference to him; she would be one of contempt were he to understand her emotions. Her beauty is much admired by the Vernons, but it has no effect on *him*. She is in high favour with her aunt altogether—because she is so little like myself, of course. She is exactly the companion for Mrs. Vernon, who dearly loves to be first, and to have all the sense and all the wit of the conversation to herself: Frederica will never eclipse her. When she first came, I was at some pains to prevent her seeing much of her aunt; but I have since relaxed, as I beleive I may depend on her observing the rules I have laid down for their discourse.

But do not imagine that with all this lenity I have for a moment given up my plan of her marriage; No, I am unalterably fixed on this point, tho' I have not yet quite decided on the manner of bringing it about. I should not chuse to have the business brought forward here, and canvassed by the wise heads of Mr. and Mrs. Vernon; and I cannot just now afford to go to Town. Miss Frederica therefore must wait a little.

Yours ever

S. VERNON

LETTER 20

Mrs. Vernon to Lady De Courcy

Churchill

We have a very unexpected guest with us at present, my dear mother. He arrived yesterday. I heard a carriage at the door, as I was sitting with my children while they dined; and supposing I should be wanted, left the nursery soon afterwards, and was half-way downstairs, when Frederica, as pale as ashes, came running up, and rushed by me into her own room. I instantly followed, and asked her what was the matter. "Oh! cried she, he is come, Sir James is come—and what am I to do?" This was no explanation; I begged her to tell me what she meant. At that moment we were interrupted by a knock at the door: it was Reginald who came, by Lady Susan's direction, to call Frederica down. "It is Mr. De Courcy, said she, colouring violently, Mama has sent for me, and I must go."

We all three went down together; and I saw my brother examining the terrified face of Frederica with surprise. In the breakfast room we found Lady Susan, and a young man of genteel appearance, whom she introduced to me by the name of Sir James Martin—the very person, as you may remember, whom it was said she had been at pains to detach from Miss Manwaring. But the conquest, it seems, was not designed for herself, or she has since transferred it to her daughter; for Sir James is now desperately in love with Frederica, and with full encouragement from Mama. The poor girl, however, I am sure, dislikes him; and tho' his person and address are very well, he appears, both to Mr. Vernon and me, a very weak young man.

Frederica looked so shy, so confused, when we entered the room, that I felt for her exceedingly. Lady Susan behaved with great attention to her visitor; and yet I thought I could perceive that she had no particular pleasure in seeing him. Sir James talked a great deal, and made many civil excuses to me for the liberty he had taken in coming to Churchill, mixing more frequent laughter with his discourse than the subject required, said many things over and over again, and told Lady Susan three times that he had seen Mrs. Johnson a few evenings before. He now and then addressed Frederica, but more frequently her mother. The poor girl sat all this time without opening her lips—her eyes cast down, and her colour varying every instant; while Reginald observed all that passed in perfect silence.

At length Lady Susan, weary I beleive of her situation, proposed walking; and we left the two gentlemen together, to put on our pelisses.

As we went upstairs, Lady Susan begged permission to attend me for a few moments in my dressing room, as she was anxious to speak with me in private. I led her thither accordingly, and as soon as the door was closed, she said, "I was never more surprised in my life than by Sir James's arrival, and the suddenness of it requires some apology to *You,* my dear sister; tho' to *me* as a mother, it is highly flattering. He is so extremely attached to my daughter that he could not exist longer without seeing her. Sir James is a young man of an amiable disposition and excellent character; a little too much of the *rattle,* perhaps, but a year or two will rectify *that,* and he is in other respects so very eligible a match for Frederica, that I have always observed his attachment with the greatest pleasure, and am persuaded that you and my brother will give the alliance your hearty approbation. I have never before mentioned the likelihood of its taking place to any one, because I thought that while Frederica continued at school it had better not be known to exist; but now, as I am convinced that Frederica is too old ever to submit to school confinement, and have therefore begun to consider her union with Sir James as not very distant, I had intended within a few days to acquaint yourself and Mr. Vernon with the whole business. I am sure, my dear sister, you will excuse my remaining silent on it so long, and agree with me that such circumstances, while they continue from any cause in suspense, cannot be too cautiously concealed. When you have the happiness of bestowing your sweet little Catherine, some years hence, on a man who in connection and character is alike unexceptionable, you will know what I feel now; tho' thank Heaven! you cannot have all my reasons for rejoicing in such an event. Catherine will be amply provided for, and not, like my Frederica, indebted to a fortunate establishment for the comforts of life."

She concluded by demanding my congratulations. I gave them somewhat awkwardly, I beleive; for in fact, the sudden disclosure of so important a matter took from me the power of speaking with any clearness. She thanked me, however, most affectionately, for my kind concern in the welfare of herself and daughter; and then said,

"I am not apt to deal in professions, my dear Mrs. Vernon, and I never had the convenient talent of affecting sensations foreign to my heart; and therefore I trust you will beleive me when I declare that, much as I had heard in your praise before I knew you, I had no idea that I should ever love you as I now do; and I must further say that your friendship towards me is more particularly gratifying because I have reason to beleive that some attempts were made to prejudice you against me. I only wish that they—whoever they are—to whom I am indebted for such kind intentions, could see the terms on which we now are together, and understand the real affection we feel for each other! But I will not detain you any longer. God bless you for your goodness to me and my girl, and continue to you all your present happiness."

What can one say of such a woman, my dear mother? Such earnestness, such solemnity of expression! and yet I cannot help suspecting the truth of everything she said.

As for Reginald, I believe he does not know what to make of the matter. When Sir James first came, he appeared all astonishment and perplexity. The folly of the young man and the confusion of Frederica entirely engrossed him; and tho' a little private discourse with Lady Susan has since had its effect, he is still hurt, I am sure, at her allowing of such a man's attentions to her daughter.

Sir James invited himself with great composure to remain here a few days—hoped we would not think it odd, was aware of its being very impertinent, but he took the liberty of a relation; and concluded by wishing, with a laugh, that he might be really one soon. Even Lady Susan seemed a little disconcerted by this forwardness; in her heart, I am persuaded, she sincerely wishes him gone.

But something must be done for this poor girl, if her feelings are such as both her uncle and I beleive them to be. She must not be sacrificed to policy or ambition; she must not be even left to suffer from the dread of it. The girl whose heart can distinguish Reginald De Courcy deserves, however he may slight her, a better fate than to be Sir James Martin's wife. As soon as I can get her alone, I will discover the real truth; but she seems to wish to avoid me. I hope this does not proceed from anything wrong, and that I shall not find out I have thought too well of her. Her behaviour to Sir James certainly speaks the greatest consciousness and embarrassment, but I see nothing in it more like encouragement.

Adieu, my dear Madam,

Yours etc.

CATH. VERNON

LETTER 21

Miss Vernon to Mr. De Courcy

Sir,

I hope you will excuse this liberty; I am forced upon it by the greatest distress, or I should be ashamed to trouble you. I am very miserable about Sir James Martin, and have no other way in the world of helping myself but by writing to you, for I am forbidden ever speaking to my uncle or aunt on the subject; and this being the case, I am afraid my applying to you will appear no better than equivocation, and as if I attended only to the letter and not the spirit of Mama's commands. But if *you* do not take my part and persuade her to break it off, I shall be half distracted, for I cannot bear him. No human being but *you* could have any chance of prevailing with her. If you will, therefore, have the unspeakable great kindness of taking my part with her, and persuading her to send Sir James away, I shall be more obliged to you than it is possible for me to express. I always disliked him from the first; it is not a sudden fancy, I assure you, Sir, I always thought him silly and impertinent and disagreable, and now he is grown worse than ever. I would rather work for my bread than marry him. I do not know how to apologise enough for this letter; I know it is taking so great a liberty; I am aware how dreadfully angry it will make Mama, but I must run the risk. I am, Sir, your most Humble Servant

F. S. V.

LETTER 22

Lady Susan to Mrs. Johnson

Churchill

This is insufferable! My dearest friend, I was never so enraged before, and must relieve myself by writing to you, who I know will enter into all my feelings. Who should come on Tuesday but Sir James Martin! Guess my astonishment and vexation— for, as you well know, I never wished him to be seen at Churchill. What a pity that you should not have known his intentions! Not content with coming, he actually invited himself to remain here a few days. I could have poisoned him; I made the best of it, however, and told my story with great success to Mrs. Vernon, who, whatever might be her real sentiments, said nothing in opposition to mine. I made a point also of Frederica's behaving civilly to Sir James, and gave her to understand that I was absolutely determined on her marrying him. She said something of her misery, but that was all. I have for some time been more particularly resolved on the match from seeing the rapid increase of her affection for Reginald, and from not feeling perfectly secure that a knowledge of *that* affection might not in the end awaken a return. Contemptible as a regard founded only on compassion must make them both in my eyes, I felt by no means assured that such might not be the consequence. It is true that Reginald had not in any degree grown cool towards me; but yet he had lately mentioned Frederica spontaneously and unnecessarily, and once had said something in praise of her person.

He was all astonishment at the appearance of my visitor, and at first observed Sir James with an attention which I was pleased to see not unmixed with jealousy; but unluckily it was impossible for me really to torment him, as Sir James, tho' extremely gallant to me, very soon made the whole party understand that his heart was devoted to my daughter.

I had no great difficulty in convincing De Courcy, when we were alone, that I was perfectly justified, all things considered, in desiring the match; and the whole business seemed most comfortably arranged. They could none of them help perceiving that Sir James was no Solomon; but I had positively forbidden Frederica's complaining to Charles Vernon or his wife, and they had therefore no pretence for interference; tho' my impertinent sister, I beleive, wanted only opportunity for doing so.

Everything, however, was going on calmly and quietly; and tho' I counted the hours of Sir James's stay, my mind was entirely satisfied with the posture of affairs. Guess, then, what I must feel at the sudden disturbance of all my schemes; and that, too, from a quarter whence I had least reason to apprehend it. Reginald came this morning into my dressing room with a very unusual solemnity of countenance, and after some preface informed me in so many words that he wished to reason with me on the impropriety and unkindness of allowing Sir James Martin to address my daughter contrary to *her* inclination. I was all amazement. When I found that he was not to be laughed out of his design, I calmly required an explanation, and begged to know by what he was impelled, and by whom commissioned to reprimand me. He then told me, mixing in his speech a few insolent compliments and ill-timed expressions of tenderness, to which I listened with perfect indifference, that my daughter had acquainted him with some circumstances concerning herself, Sir James, and me, which gave him great uneasiness.

In short, I found that she had in the first place actually written to him to request his interference, and that on receiving her letter, he had conversed with her on the subject of it, in order to understand the particulars, and assure himself of her real wishes!

I have not a doubt but that the girl took this opportunity of making downright love to him. I am convinced of it from the manner in which he spoke of her. Much good may such love do him! I shall ever despise the man who can be gratified by the passion which he never wished to inspire, nor solicited the avowal of. I shall always detest them both. He can have no true regard for me, or he would not have listened to her; and she, with her little rebellious heart and indelicate feelings, to throw herself into the protection of a young man with whom she has scarcely ever exchanged two words before. I am equally confounded at *her* impudence and *his* credulity. How dared he beleive what she told him in my disfavour! Ought he not to have felt assured that I must have unanswerable motives for all that I had done! Where was his reliance on my sense or goodness then? Where the resentment which true love would have dictated against the person defaming me—that person, too, a chit, a child, without talent or education, whom he had been always taught to despise?

I was calm for some time; but the greatest degree of forbearance may be overcome, and I hope I was afterwards sufficiently keen. He endeavoured, long endeavoured, to soften my resentment; but that woman is a fool indeed who, while insulted by accusation, can be worked on by compliments. At length he left me, as deeply provoked as myself; and he shewed his anger *more*. I was quite cool, but he gave way to the most violent indignation. I may therefore expect it will the sooner subside; and perhaps his may be vanished forever, while mine will be found still fresh and implacable.

He is now shut up in his apartment, whither I heard him go on leaving mine. How unpleasant, one would think, must his reflections be! But some people's feelings are incomprehensible. I have not yet tranquillized myself enough to see Frederica. *She* shall not soon forget the occurrences of this day; she shall find that she has poured forth her tender tale of love in vain, and exposed herself forever to the contempt of the whole world, and the severest resentment of her injured mother.

Yours affectionately

S. VERNON

LETTER 23

Mrs. Vernon to Lady De Courcy

Churchill

Let me congratulate you, my dearest mother. The affair which has given us so much anxiety is drawing to a happy conclusion. Our prospect is most delightful; and since matters have now taken so favourable a turn, I am quite sorry that I ever imparted my apprehensions to you; for the pleasure of learning that the danger is over is perhaps dearly purchased by all that you have previously suffered.

I am so much agitated by delight that I can scarcely hold a pen; but am determined to send you a few short lines by James, that you may have some explanation of what must so greatly astonish you, as that Reginald should be returning to Parklands.

I was sitting about half an hour ago with Sir James in the breakfast parlour, when my brother called me out of the room. I instantly saw that something was the matter; his complexion was raised, and he spoke with great emotion. You know his eager manner, my dear Madam, when his mind is interested.

"Catherine, said he, I am going home today; I am sorry to leave you, but I must go. It is a great while since I have seen my father and mother. I am going to send James forward with my Hunters immediately; if you have any letter, therefore, he can take it. I shall not be at home myself till Wednesday or Thursday, as I shall go through London, where I have business. But before I leave you, he continued, speaking in a lower voice, and with still greater energy, I must warn you of one thing—do not let Frederica Vernon be made unhappy by that Martin. He wants to marry her—her mother promotes the match—but *she* cannot endure the idea of it. Be assured that I speak from the fullest conviction of the truth of what I say; I *know* that Frederica is made wretched by Sir James' continuing here. She is a sweet girl, and deserves a better fate. Send him away immediately. *He* is only a fool—but what her mother can mean, Heaven only knows! Good-bye, he added, shaking my hand with earnestness—I do not know when you will see me again; but remember what I tell you of Frederica; you *must* make it your business to see justice done her. She is an amiable girl, and has a very superior mind to what we have ever given her credit for."

He then left me, and ran upstairs. I would not try to stop him, for I know what his feelings must be; the nature of mine, as I listened to him, I need not attempt to describe. For a minute or two, I remained in the same spot, overpowered by wonder—of a most agreable sort indeed; yet it required some consideration to be tranquilly happy.

In about ten minutes after my return to the parlour, Lady Susan entered the room. I concluded, of course, that she and Reginald had been quarrelling, and looked with anxious curiosity for a confirmation of my beleif in her face. Mistress of deceit, however, she appeared perfectly unconcerned, and after chatting on indifferent subjects for a short time, said to me, "I find from Wilson that we are going to lose Mr. De Courcy—is it true that he leaves Churchill this morning?" I replied that it was. "He told us nothing of all this last night," said she, laughing, "or even this morning at breakfast; but perhaps he did not know it himself. Young men are often hasty in their resolutions—and not more sudden in forming than unsteady in keeping them. I should not be surprised if he were to change his mind at last, and not go."

She soon afterwards left the room. I trust, however, my dear mother, that we have no reason to fear an alteration of his present plan; things have gone too far. They must have quarrelled, and about Frederica too. Her calmness astonishes me. What delight will be yours in seeing him again, in seeing him still worthy of your esteem, still capable of forming your happiness!

When I next write, I shall be able, I hope, to tell you that Sir James is gone, Lady Susan vanquished, and Frederica at peace. We have much to do, but it shall be done. I am all impatience to hear how this astonishing change was effected. I finish as I began, with the warmest congratulations.

Yours ever,
CATH. VERNON

LETTER 24

From the same to the same

Churchill

Little did I imagine, my dear mother, when I sent off my last letter, that the delightful perturbation of spirits I was then in would undergo so speedy, so melancholy a reverse! I never can sufficiently regret that I wrote to you at all. Yet who could have foreseen what has happened? My dear mother, every hope which but two hours ago made me so happy is vanished. The quarrel between Lady Susan and Reginald is made up, and we are all as we were before. One point only is gained; Sir James Martin is dismissed. What are we now to look forward to? I am indeed disappointed. Reginald was all but gone; his horse was ordered and all but brought to the door! Who would not have felt safe?

For half an hour I was in momentary expectation of his departure. After I had sent off my letter to you, I went to Mr. Vernon and sat with him in his room, talking over the whole matter. I then determined to look for Frederica, whom I had not seen since breakfast. I met her on the stairs, and saw that she was crying.

"My dear aunt," said she, "he is going, Mr. De Courcy is going, and it is all my fault. I am afraid you will be angry, but indeed I had no idea it would end so."

"My love," replied I, "do not think it necessary to apologize to me on that account. I shall feel myself under an obligation to anyone who is the means of sending my brother home; because (recollecting myself) I know my father wants very much to see him. But what is it that *you* have done to occasion all this?"

She blushed deeply as she answered, "I was so unhappy about Sir James that I could not help—I have done something very wrong I know—but you have not an idea of the misery I have been in, and Mama had ordered me never to speak to you or my uncle about it, and—" "You therefore spoke to my brother, to engage *his* interference," said I, to save her the explanation. "No—but I wrote to him. I did indeed. I got up this morning before it was light—I was two hours about it—and when my letter was done, I thought I never should have courage to give it. After breakfast, however, as I was going to my room, I met him in the passage, and then, as I knew that everything must depend on that moment, I forced myself to give it. He was so good as to take it immediately. I dared not look at him, and ran away directly. I was in such a fright that I could hardly breathe. My dear aunt, you do not know how miserable I have been."

"Frederica," said I, "you ought to have told *me* all your distresses. You would have found in me a friend always ready to assist you. Do you think that your uncle and I should not have espoused your cause as warmly as my brother?"

"Indeed, I did not doubt your goodness," said she, colouring again, "but I thought Mr. De Courcy could do anything with my mother; but I was mistaken: they have had a dreadful quarrel about it, and he is going. Mama will never forgive me, and I shall be worse off than ever." "No, you shall not," replied I. "In such a point as this, your mother's prohibition ought not to have prevented your speaking to me on the subject. She has no right to make you unhappy, and she shall *not* do it. Your applying, however, to Reginald can be productive only of good to all parties. I beleive it is best as it is. Depend upon it that you shall not be made unhappy any longer."

At that moment, how great was my astonishment at seeing Reginald come out of Lady Susan's dressing room. My heart misgave me instantly. His confusion on seeing me was very evident. Frederica immediately disappeared. "Are you going?" said I. "You will find Mr. Vernon in his own room." "No, Catherine," replied he, "I am *not* going. Will you let me speak to you a moment?"

We went into my room. "I find," continued he, his confusion increasing as he spoke, "that I have been acting with my usual foolish impetuosity. I have entirely misunderstood Lady Susan, and was on the point of leaving the house under a false impression of her conduct. There has been some very great mistake— we have been all mistaken, I fancy. Frederica does not know her mother—Lady Susan means nothing but her good—but Frederica will not make a friend of her. Lady Susan therefore does not always know what will make her daughter happy. Besides, *I* could have no right to interfere—Miss Vernon was mistaken in applying to me. In short, Catherine, everything has gone wrong—but it is now all happily settled. Lady Susan, I beleive, wishes to speak to you about it, if you are at leisure."

"Certainly;" replied I, deeply sighing at the recital of so lame a story. I made no comments, however, for words would have been vain. Reginald was glad to get away; and I went to Lady Susan; curious, indeed, to hear her account of it.

"Did I not tell you," said she, with a smile, "that your brother would not leave us after all?" "You did, indeed," replied I, very gravely, "but I flattered myself that you would be mistaken." "I should not have hazarded such an opinion," returned she, "if it had not at that moment occurred [to] me that his resolution of going might be occasioned by a conversation in which we had been this morning engaged, and which had ended very much to his dissatisfaction, from our not rightly understanding each other's meaning. This idea struck me at the moment, and I instantly determined that an accidental dispute, in which I might probably be as much to blame as himself, should not deprive you of your brother. If you remember, I left the room almost immediately. I was resolved to lose no time in clearing up those mistakes as far as I could. The case was this: Frederica had set herself violently against marrying Sir James"—"And can your Ladyship wonder that she should?" cried I, with some warmth; "Frederica has an excellent understanding, and Sir James has none." "I am at least very far from regretting it, my dear sister," said she; "on the contrary, I am grateful for so favourable a sign of my daughter's sense. Sir James is certainly under par—(his boyish manners make him appear the worse)—and had Frederica possessed the penetration, the abilities which I could have wished in my daughter, or had I even known her to possess as much as she does, I should not have been anxious for the match." "It is odd that you should alone be ignorant of your daughter's sense." "Frederica never does justice to herself; her manners are shy and childish. She is besides afraid of me; she scarcely loves me. During her poor father's life she was a spoilt child; the severity which it has since been necessary for me to

shew has alienated her affection; neither has she any of that brilliancy of intellect, that genius, or vigour of mind which will force
itself forward." "Say rather that she has been unfortunate in her
education!" "Heaven knows, my dearest Mrs. Vernon, how fully
I am aware of *that*; but I would wish to forget every circumstance that might throw blame on the memory of one whose
name is sacred with me."

Here she pretended to cry; I was out of patience with her.
"But what," said I, "was your Ladyship going to tell me about
your disagreement with my brother?" "It originated in an action
of my daughter's which equally marks her want of judgement
and the unfortunate dread of me I have been mentioning—she
wrote to Mr. De Courcy." "I know she did; you had forbidden
her speaking to Mr. Vernon or to me on the cause of her distress;
what could she do, therefore, but apply to my brother?" "Good
God!" she exclaimed, "what an opinion you must have of me!
Can you possibly suppose that I was aware of her unhappiness?
that it was my object to make my own child miserable, and that
I had forbidden her speaking to you on the subject from fear of
your interrupting the diabolical scheme? Do you think me des-
titute of every honest, every natural feeling? Am I capable of
consigning *her* to everlasting misery whose welfare it is my first
earthly duty to promote?" "The idea is horrible. What, then, was
your intention when you insisted on her silence?" "Of what use,
my dear sister, could be any application to you, however the
affair might stand? Why should I subject you to entreaties which
I refused to attend to myself? Neither for your sake, for hers,
nor for my own, could such a thing be desirable. When my own
resolution was taken, I could not wish for the interference, however friendly, of another person. I was mistaken, it is true, but I
beleived myself right." "But what was this mistake to which your
Ladyship so often alludes? From whence arose so astonishing a
misconception of your daughter's feelings? Did you not know
that she disliked Sir James?" "I knew that he was not absolutely
the man she would have chosen, but I was persuaded that her
objections to him did not arise from any perception of his defi-
ciency. You must not question me, however, my dear sister, too
minutely on this point," continued she, taking me affectionately

by the hand; "I honestly own that there is something to conceal. Frederica makes me very unhappy. Her applying to Mr. De Courcy hurt me particularly." "What is it you mean to infer," said I, "by this appearance of mystery? If you think your daughter at all attached to Reginald, her objecting to Sir James could not less deserve to be attended to than if the cause of her objecting had been a consciousness of his folly; and why should your Ladyship, at any rate, quarrel with my brother for an interference which you must know it is not in his nature to refuse when urged in such a manner?"

"His disposition, you know, is warm, and he came to expostulate with me; his compassion all alive for this ill-used girl, this heroine in distress! We misunderstood each other: he beleived me more to blame than I really was; I considered his interference less excusable than I now find it. I have a real regard for him, and was beyond expression mortified to find it, as I thought, so ill bestowed. We were both warm, and of course both to blame. His resolution of leaving Churchill is consistent with his general eagerness. When I understood his intention, however, and at the same time began to think that we had been perhaps equally mistaken in each other's meaning, I resolved to have an explanation before it was too late. For any member of your family I must always feel a degree of affection, and I own it would have sensibly hurt me if my acquaintance with Mr. De Courcy had ended so gloomily. I have now only to say farther, that as I am convinced of Frederica's having a reasonable dislike to Sir James, I shall instantly inform him that he must give up all hope of her. I reproach myself for having ever, tho' innocently, made her unhappy on that score. She shall have all the retribution in my power to make; if she value her own happiness as much as I do, if she judge wisely, and command herself as she ought, she may now be easy. Excuse me, my dearest sister, for thus trespassing on your time, but I owed it to my own character; and after this explanation I trust I am in no danger of sinking in your opinion."

I could have said, "Not much, indeed"; but I left her almost in silence. It was the greatest stretch of forbearance I could practise. I could not have stopped myself had I begun. Her assurance, her deceit—but I will not allow myself to dwell on them; they will strike you sufficiently. My heart sickens within me.

As soon as I was tolerably composed I returned to the parlour. Sir James's carriage was at the door, and he, merry as usual, soon afterwards took his leave. How easily does her Ladyship encourage or dismiss a lover!

In spite of this release, Frederica still looks unhappy, still fearful, perhaps, of her mother's anger; and tho' dreading my brother's departure, jealous, it may be, of his staying. I see how closely she observes him and Lady Susan. Poor girl, I have now no hope for her. There is not a chance of her affection being returned. He thinks very differently of her from what he used to do, he does her some justice, but his reconciliation with her mother precludes every dearer hope.

Prepare, my dear Madam, for the worst. The probability of their marrying is surely heightened. He is more securely hers than ever. When that wretched event takes place, Frederica must wholly belong to us.

I am thankful that my last letter will precede this by so little, as every moment that you can be saved from feeling a joy which leads only to disappointment is of consequence.

Yours ever,
CATH. VERNON

LETTER 25

Lady Susan to Mrs. Johnson

Churchill

I call on you, dear Alicia, for congratulations: I am again myself;—gay and triumphant! When I wrote to you the other day I was, in truth, in high irritation, and with ample cause. Nay, I know not whether I ought to be quite tranquil now, for I have had more trouble in restoring peace than I ever intended to submit to. This Reginald has a proud spirit of his own! a spirit, too, resulting from a fancied sense of superior integrity, which is peculiarly insolent! I shall not easily forgive him, I assure you. He was actually on the point of leaving Churchill! I had scarcely concluded my last, when Wilson brought me word of it. I found, therefore, that something must be done; for I did not chuse to leave my character at the mercy of a man whose passions are so violent and resentful. It would have been trifling with my reputation to allow of his departing with such an impression in my disfavour; in this light, condescension was necessary.

I sent Wilson to say that I desired to speak with him before he went; he came immediately. The angry emotions which had marked every feature when we last parted were partially subdued. He seemed astonished at the summons, and looked as if half wishing and half fearing to be softened by what I might say.

If my countenance expressed what I aimed at, it was composed and dignified—and yet with a degree of pensiveness which might convince him that I was not quite happy. "I beg your pardon Sir, for the liberty I have taken in sending for you, said I; but as I have just learnt your intention of leaving this place to-day, I feel it my duty to entreat that you will not on my account shorten your visit here even an hour. I am perfectly aware that after what has passed between us it would ill suit the feelings of either to remain longer in the same house: so very great, so total a change from the intimacy of friendship must render any future intercourse the severest punishment; and your resolution of quitting Churchill is undoubtedly in unison with our situation, and with those lively feelings which I know you to possess. But at the same time it is not for me to suffer such a sacrifice as it must be to leave relations to whom you are so much attached and are so dear. My remaining here cannot give that pleasure to Mr. and Mrs. Vernon which your society must; and my visit has already perhaps been too long. My removal, therefore, which must at any rate take place soon, may with perfect convenience be hastened; and I make it my particular request that I may not in any way be instrumental in separating a family so affectionately attached to each other. Where *I* go is of no consequence to anyone; of very little to myself; but *you* are of importance to all your connections." Here I concluded, and I hope you will be satisfied with my speech. Its effect on Reginald justifies some portion of vanity, for it was no less favourable than instantaneous. Oh, how delightful it was to watch the variations of his countenance while I spoke! to see the struggle between returning tenderness and the remains of displeasure. There is something agreable in feelings so easily worked on; not that I envy him their possession, nor would, for the world, have such myself; but they are very convenient when one wishes to influence the passions of another. And yet this Reginald, whom a very few words from me softened at once into the utmost submission, and rendered more tractable, more attached, more devoted than ever, would have left me in the first angry swelling of his proud heart without deigning to seek an explanation.

Humbled as he now is, I cannot forgive him such an instance of pride, and am doubtful whether I ought not to punish him by dismissing him at once after this reconciliation, or by marrying and teizing him for ever. But these measures are each too violent to be adopted without some deliberation; at present my thoughts are fluctuating between various schemes. I have many things to compass: I must punish Frederica, and pretty severely too, for her application to Reginald; I must punish him for receiving it so favourably, and for the rest of his conduct. I must torment my sister-in-law for the insolent triumph of her look and manner since Sir James has been dismissed; for in reconciling Reginald to me, I was not able to save that ill-fated young man;—and I must make myself amends for the humiliation to which I have stooped within these few days. To effect all this I have various plans. I have also an idea of being soon in Town; and whatever may be my determination as to the rest, I shall probably put *that* project in execution—for London will always be the fairest field of action, however my views may be directed; and at any rate I shall there be rewarded by your society, and a little dissipation, for a ten weeks' penance at Churchill.

I beleive I owe it to my own character to complete the match between my daughter and Sir James, after having so long intended it. Let me know your opinion on this point. Flexibility of mind, a disposition easily biassed by others, is an attribute which you know I am not very desirous of obtaining; nor has Frederica any claim to the indulgence of her notions at the expense of her mother's inclination. Her idle love for Reginald, too! It is surely my duty to discourage such romantic nonsense.

All things considered, therefore, it seems incumbent on me to take her to Town and marry her immediately to Sir James.

When my own will is effected contrary to his, I shall have some credit in being on good terms with Reginald, which at present, in fact, I have not; for tho' he is still in my power, I have given up the very article by which our quarrel was produced, and at best the honour of victory is doubtful.

Send me your opinion on all these matters, my dear Alicia, and let me know whether you can get lodgings to suit me within a short distance of you.

Your most attached
S. VERNON

LETTER 26

Mrs. Johnson to Lady Susan

Edward St.

I am gratified by your reference, and this is my advice: that you come to Town yourself, without loss of time, but that you leave Frederica behind. It would surely be much more to the purpose to get yourself well established by marrying Mr. De Courcy, than to irritate him and the rest of his family by making her marry Sir James. You should think more of yourself and less of your daughter. She is not of a disposition to do you credit in the world, and seems precisely in her proper place at Churchill with the Vernons. But you *are* fitted for society, and it is shameful to have you exiled from it. Leave Frederica, therefore, to punish herself for the plague she has given you, by indulging that romantic tender-heartedness which will always ensure her misery enough, and come yourself to Town as soon as you can.

I have another reason for urging this:

Manwaring came to Town last week, and has contrived, in spite of Mr. Johnson, to make opportunities of seeing me. He is absolutely miserable about you, and jealous to such a degree of De Courcy, that it would be highly unadvisable for them to meet at present. And yet, if you do not allow him to see you here, I cannot answer for his not committing same great imprudence—

such as going to Churchill, for instance, which would be dreadful! Besides, if you take my advice, and resolve to marry De Courcy, it will be indispensably necessary for you to get Manwaring out of the way; and you only can have influence enough to send him back to his wife.

I have still another motive for your coming: Mr. Johnson leaves London next Tuesday; he is going for his health to Bath, where, if the waters are favourable to his constitution and my wishes, he will be laid up with the gout many weeks. During his absence we shall be able to choose our own society, and to have true enjoyment. I would ask you to Edward Street, but that he once forced from me a kind of promise never to invite you to my house; nothing but my being in the utmost distress for money should have extorted it from me. I can get you, however, a nice drawing-room-apartment in Upper Seymour St, and we may be always together there or here; for I consider my promise to Mr. Johnson as comprehending only (at least in his absence) your not sleeping in the house.

Poor Manwaring gives me such histories of his wife's jealousy! Silly woman, to expect constancy from so charming a man! But she always was silly; intolerably so, in marrying him at all. She, the heiress of a large fortune, he without a shilling! *One* title, I know, she might have had, besides baronets. Her folly in forming the connection was so great that tho' Mr. Johnson was her guardian, and I do not in general share his feelings, I never can forgive her.

Adieu, Yours, ALICIA

LETTER 27

Mrs. Vernon to Lady De Courcy

Churchill

This letter, my dear mother, will be brought you by Reginald. His long visit is about to be concluded at last, but I fear the separation takes place too late to do us any good. *She* is going to London to see her particular friend, Mrs. Johnson. It was at first her intention that Frederica should accompany her, for the benefit of masters, but we over-ruled her there. Frederica was wretched in the idea of going, and I could not bear to have her at the mercy of her mother; not all the masters in London could compensate for the ruin of her comfort. I should have feared, too, for her health, and for everything but her principles—*there* I beleive she is not to be injured by her mother, or all her mother's friends; but with those friends (a very bad set, I doubt not) she must have mixed, or have been left in total solitude, and I can hardly tell which would have been worse for her. If she is with her mother, moreover, she must, alas! in all probability be with Reginald—and that would be the greatest evil of all.

Here we shall in time be in peace. Our regular employments, our books and conversation, with exercise, the children, and every domestic pleasure in my power to procure her, will, I trust, gradually overcome this youthful attachment. I should not have a doubt of it, were she slighted for any other woman in the world than her own mother.

How long Lady Susan will be in Town, or whether she returns here again, I know not. I could not be cordial in my invitation; but if she chuses to come, no want of cordiality on my part will keep her away.

I could not help asking Reginald if he intended being in Town this winter, as soon as I found her Ladyship's steps would be bent thither; and tho' he professed himself quite undetermined, there was something in his look and voice as he spoke which contradicted his words. I have done with lamentation. I look upon the event as so far decided that I resign myself to it in despair. If he leaves you soon for London, everything will be concluded.

Yours affectionately

C. VERNON

LETTER 28

Mrs. Johnson to Lady Susan

Edward St.

My dearest Friend,

I write in the greatest distress; the most unfortunate event has just taken place. Mr. Johnson has hit on the most effectual manner of plaguing us all. He had heard, I imagine, by some means or other, that you were soon to be in London, and immediately contrived to have such an attack of the gout as must at least delay his journey to Bath, if not wholly prevent it. I am persuaded the gout is brought on or kept off at pleasure; it was the same when I wanted to join the Hamiltons to the Lakes; and three years ago, when *I* had a fancy for Bath, nothing could induce him to have a gouty symptom.

I have received yours, and have engaged the lodgings in consequence. I am pleased to find that my letter had so much effect on you, and that De Courcy is certainly your own. Let me hear from you as soon as you arrive, and in particular tell me what you mean to do with Manwaring. It is impossible to say when I shall be able to see you; my confinement must be great. It is such an abominable trick to be ill here, instead of at Bath, that I can scarcely command myself at all. At Bath, his old aunts would have nursed him, but here it all falls upon me—and he bears pain with such patience that I have not the common excuse for losing my temper.

Yours ever,
ALICIA

LETTER 29

Lady Susan to Mrs. Johnson

Upper Seymour St.

My dear Alicia
There needed not this last fit of the gout to make me detest Mr. Johnson, but now the extent of my aversion is not to be estimated. To have you confined as nurse in his apartment! My dear Alicia, of what a mistake were you guilty in marrying a man of his age! just old enough to be formal, ungovernable, and to have the gout—too old to be agreable, too young to die.

I arrived last night about five, and had scarcely swallowed my dinner when Manwaring made his appearance. I will not dissemble what real pleasure his sight afforded me, nor how strongly I felt the contrast between his person and manners and those of Reginald, to the infinite disadvantage of the latter. For an hour or two I was even staggered in my resolution of marrying him—and tho' this was too idle and nonsensical an idea to remain long on my mind, I do not feel very eager for the conclusion of my marriage, nor look forward with much impatience to the time when Reginald, according to our agreement, is to be in Town. I shall probably put off his arrival under some pretence or other. He must not come till Manwaring is gone.

I am still doubtful at times as to marriage. If the old man would die, I might not hesitate; but a state of dependence on the caprice of Sir Reginald will not suit the freedom of my spirit; and if I resolve to wait for that event, I shall have excuse enough at present, in having been scarcely ten months a widow.

I have not given Manwaring any hint of my intention—or allowed him to consider my acquaintance with Reginald as more than the commonest flirtation, and he is tolerably appeased. Adieu, till we meet; I am enchanted with my lodgings.

Yours ever,
S. VERNON

LETTER 30

Lady Susan to Mr. De Courcy

Upper Seymour St.

I have received your letter, and tho' I do not attempt to conceal that I am gratified by your impatience for the hour of meeting, I yet feel myself under the necessity of delaying that hour beyond the time originally fixed. Do not think me unkind for such an exercise of my power, nor accuse me of instability without first hearing my reasons. In the course of my journey from Churchill, I had ample leisure for reflection on the present state of our affairs, and every review has served to convince me that they require a delicacy and cautiousness of conduct to which we have hitherto been too little attentive. We have been hurried on by our feelings to a degree of precipitance which ill accords with the claims of our friends or the opinion of the world. We have been unguarded in forming this hasty engagement, but we must not complete the imprudence by ratifying it while there is so much reason to fear the connection would be opposed by those friends on whom you depend.

It is not for us to blame any expectations on your father's side of your marrying to advantage; where possessions are so extensive as those of your family, the wish of increasing them, if not strictly reasonable, is too common to excite surprise or resentment. He has a right to require a woman of fortune in his daughter in law, and I am sometimes quarrelling with myself for suffering you to form a connection so imprudent; but the influence of reason is often acknowledged too late by those who feel like me.

I have now been but a few months a widow; and, however little indebted to my husband's memory for any happiness derived from him during a union of some years, I cannot forget that the indelicacy of so early a second marriage must subject me to the censure of the world, and incur what would be still more insupportable, the displeasure of Mr. Vernon. I might perhaps harden myself in time against the injustice of general reproach, but the loss of *his* valued esteem I am, as you well know, ill-fitted to endure; and when to this may be added the consciousness of having injured you with your family, how am I to support myself? With feelings so poignant as mine, the conviction of having divided the son from his parents, would make me, even with *you*, the most miserable of beings.

It will surely, therefore, be advisable to delay our union, to delay it till appearances are more promising, till affairs have taken a more favourable turn. To assist us in such a resolution, I feel that absence will be necessary. We must not meet. Cruel as this sentence may appear, the necessity of pronouncing it, which can alone reconcile it to myself, will be evident to you when you have considered our situation in the light in which I have found myself imperiously obliged to place it. You may be—you must be—well assured that nothing but the strongest conviction of duty could induce me to wound my own feelings by urging a lengthened separation, and of insensibility to yours you will hardly suspect me. Again, therefore, I say that we ought not, we must not yet meet. By a removal for some months from each other, we shall tranquillize the sisterly fears of Mrs. Vernon, who, accustomed herself to the enjoyment of riches, considers fortune as necessary everywhere, and whose sensibilities are not of a nature to comprehend ours.

Let me hear from you soon—very soon. Tell me that you submit to my arguments, and do not reproach me for using such. I cannot bear reproaches: my spirits are not so high as to need being repressed. I must endeavour to seek amusement abroad, and fortunately many of my friends are in town—among them the Manwarings; you know how sincerely I regard both husband and wife.

I am ever, faithfully yours

S. VERNON

LETTER 31

Lady Susan to Mrs. Johnson

Upper Seymour St.

My dear Friend,

That tormenting creature Reginald is here. My letter, which was intended to keep him longer in the country, has hastened him to Town. Much as I wish him away, however, I cannot help being pleased with such a proof of attachment. He is devoted to me, heart and soul. He will carry this note himself, which is to serve as an introduction to you, with whom he longs to be acquainted. Allow him to spend the evening with you, that I may be in no danger of his returning here. I have told him that I am not quite well, and must be alone; and should he call again there might be confusion, for it is impossible to be sure of servants. Keep him, therefore, I entreat you, in Edward St. You will not find him a heavy companion, and I allow you to flirt with him as much as you like. At the same time do not forget my real interest; say all that you can to convince him that I shall be quite wretched if he remains here; you know my reasons—propriety, and so forth. I would urge them more myself, but that I am impatient to be rid of him, as Manwaring comes within half an hour. Adieu,

S. V.

LETTER 32

Mrs. Johnson to Lady Susan

Edward St.

My dear Creature,

I am in agonies, and know not what to do, nor what *you* can do. Mr. De Courcy arrived just when he should not. Mrs. Manwaring had that instant entered the house, and forced herself into her guardian's presence, tho' I did not know a syllable of it till afterwards, for I was out when both she and Reginald came, or I would have sent him away at all events; but *she* was shut up with Mr. Johnson, while *he* waited in the drawing room for me. She arrived yesterday in pursuit of her husband; but perhaps you know this already from himself. She came to this house to entreat my husband's interference, and before I could be aware of it, everything that you could wish to be concealed was known to him, and unluckily she had wormed out of Manwaring's servant that he had visited you every day since your being in Town, and had just watched him to your door herself! What could I do? Facts are such horrid things! All is by this time known to De Courcy, who is now alone with Mr. Johnson. Do not accuse me; indeed, it was impossible to prevent it. Mr. Johnson has for some time suspected De Courcy of intending to marry you, and would speak with him alone as soon as he knew him to be in the house.

That detestable Mrs. Manwaring, who, for your comfort, has fretted herself thinner and uglier than ever, is still here, and they have been all closeted together. What can be done? If Manwaring is now with you, he had better be gone. At any rate, I hope he will plague his wife more than ever. With anxious wishes,

Yours faithfully
ALICIA

LETTER 33

Lady Susan to Mrs. Johnson

Upper Seymour St

This eclaircissement is rather provoking. How unlucky that you should have been from home! I thought myself sure of you at 7. I am undismayed, however. Do not torment yourself with fears on my account; depend on it, I can make my story good with Reginald. Manwaring is just gone; he brought me the news of his wife's arrival. Silly woman, what does she expect by such manoeuvres? Yet I wish she had staid quietly at Langford.

Reginald will be a little enraged at first, but by tomorrow's dinner everything will be well again.

Adieu.

S. V.

LETTER 34

Mr. De Courcy to Lady Susan

Hotel

I write only to bid you farewell. The spell is removed; I see you as you are. Since we parted yesterday, I have received from indisputable authority such an history of you as must bring the most mortifying conviction of the imposition I have been under, and the absolute necessity of an immediate and eternal separation from you. You cannot doubt to what I allude. Langford— Langford—that word will be sufficient. I received my information in Mr. Johnson's house, from Mrs. Manwaring herself.

You know how I have loved you; you can intimately judge of my present feelings; but I am not so weak as to find indulgence in describing them to a woman who will glory in having excited their anguish, but whose affection they have never been able to gain.

R. DE COURCY

LETTER 35

Lady Susan to Mr. De Courcy

Upper Seymour St.

I will not attempt to describe my astonishment in reading the note this moment received from you. I am bewildered in my endeavours to form some rational conjecture of what Mrs. Manwaring can have told you, to occasion so extraordinary a change in your sentiments. Have I not explained everything to you with respect to myself which could bear a doubtful meaning, and which the ill-nature of the world had interpreted to my discredit? What can you *now* have heard to stagger your esteem for me? Have I ever had a concealment from you? Reginald, you agitate me beyond expression. I cannot suppose that the old story of Mrs. Manwaring's jealousy can be revived again, or at least be *listened* to again. Come to me immediately, and explain what is at present absolutely incomprehensible. Beleive me, the single word of *Langford* is not of such potent intelligence as to supersede the necessity of more. If we *are* to part, it will at least be handsome to take your personal leave. But I have little heart to jest; in truth, I am serious enough—for to be sunk, tho' but for an hour, in your esteem is an humiliation to which I know not how to submit. I shall count every minute till your arrival.

S. V.

LETTER 36

Mr. De Courcy to Lady Susan

Hotel

Why would you write to me? Why do you require particulars? But since it must be so, I am obliged to declare that all the accounts of your misconduct during the life and since the death of Mr. Vernon, which had reached me, in common with the world in general, and gained my entire belief before I saw you, but which you, by the exertion of your perverted abilities had made me resolve to disallow, have been unanswerably proved to me. Nay, more, I am assured that a connection of which I had never before entertained a thought, has for some time existed, and still continues to exist, between you and the man whose family you robbed of its peace, in return for the hospitality with which you were received into it! That you have corresponded with him ever since your leaving Langford—not with his wife—but with him—and that he now visits you every day. Can you, dare you deny it? And all this at the time when I was an encouraged, an accepted lover! From what have I not escaped! I have only to be grateful. Far from me be all complaint, and every sigh of regret. My own folly had endangered me, my preservation I owe to the kindness, the integrity of another. But the unfortunate Mrs. Manwaring, whose agonies while she related the past seemed to threaten her reason—how is *she* to be consoled?

After such a discovery as this, you will scarcely affect further wonder at my meaning in bidding you adieu. My understanding is at length restored, and teaches me no less to abhor the artifices which had subdued me than to despise myself for the weakness on which their strength was founded.

R. DE COURCY

LETTER 37

Lady Susan to Mr. De Courcy

Upper Seymour St.

I am satisfied—and will trouble you no more when these few lines are dismissed. The engagement which you were eager to form a fortnight ago is no longer compatible with your views, and I rejoice to find that the prudent advice of your parents has not been given in vain. Your restoration to peace will, I doubt not, speedily follow this act of filial obedience, and I flatter myself with the hope of surviving *my* share in this disappointment.

S. V.

LETTER 38

Mrs. Johnson to Lady Susan

Edward St.

I am grieved, tho' I cannot be astonished, at your rupture with Mr. De Courcy; he has just informed Mr. Johnson of it by letter. He leaves London, he says, to-day. Be assured that I partake in all your feelings, and do not be angry if I say that our intercourse, even by letter, must soon be given up. It makes me miserable—but Mr. Johnson vows that if I persist in the connection, he will settle in the country for the rest of his life—and you know it is impossible to submit to such an extremity while any other alternative remains.

You have heard of course that the Manwarings are to part, and I am afraid Mrs. M. will come home to us again; but she is still so fond of her husband, and frets so much about him, that perhaps she may not live long.

Miss Manwaring is just come to Town to be with her aunt, and they say that she declares she will have Sir James Martin before she leaves London again. If I were you, I would certainly get him myself. I had almost forgot to give you my opinion of Mr. De Courcy, I am really delighted with him; he is full as handsome, I think, as Manwaring, and with such an open, good-humoured countenance that one cannot help loving him at first sight. Mr. Johnson and he are the greatest friends in the world. Adieu, my dearest Susan. I wish matters did not go so perversely. That unlucky visit to Langford! But I dare say you did all for the best, and there is no defying destiny.

Your sincerely attached

ALICIA

LETTER 39

Lady Susan to Mrs. Johnson

Upper Seymour St.

My dear Alicia

I yeild to the necessity which parts us. Under such circumstances you could not act otherwise. Our friendship cannot be impaired by it, and in happier times, when your situation is as independent as mine, it will unite us again in the same intimacy as ever. For this I shall impatiently wait; and meanwhile can safely assure you that I never was more at ease, or better satisfied with myself and everything about me than at the present hour. Your husband I abhor—Reginald I despise—and I am secure of never seeing either again. Have I not reason to rejoice? Manwaring is more devoted to me than ever; and were he at liberty, I doubt if I could resist even matrimony offered by *him*. This event, if his wife live with you, it may be in your power to hasten. The violence of her feelings, which must wear her out, may be easily kept in irritation. I rely on your friendship for this. I am now satisfied that I never could have brought myself to marry Reginald; and am equally determined that Frederica never *shall*. To-morrow I shall fetch her from Churchill, and let Maria Manwaring tremble for the consequence. Frederica shall be Sir James's wife before she quits my house. *She* may whimper, and the Vernons may storm; I regard them not. I am tired of submitting my will to the caprices of others—of resigning my own judgement in deference to those to whom I owe no duty, and for whom I feel no respect. I have given up too much, have been too easily worked on; but Frederica shall now find the difference.

Adieu, dearest of Friends. May the next gouty attack be more favourable! And may you always regard me as unalterably yours

S. VERNON

LETTER 40

Lady De Courcy to Mrs. Vernon

Parklands

My dear Catherine

I have charming news for you, and if I had not sent off my letter this morning, you might have been spared the vexation of knowing of Reginald's being gone to Town, for he is returned, Reginald is returned, not to ask our consent to his marrying Lady Susan, but to tell us they are parted forever! He has been only an hour in the house, and I have not been able to learn particulars, for he is so very low that I have not the heart to ask questions; but I hope we shall soon know all. This is the most joyful hour he has ever given us since the day of his birth. Nothing is wanting but to have you here, and it is our particular wish and entreaty that you would come to us as soon as you can. You have owed us a visit many long weeks. I hope nothing will make it inconvenient to Mr. Vernon, and pray bring all my grandchildren; and your dear neice is included, of course; I long to see her. It has been a sad, heavy winter hitherto, without Reginald, and seeing nobody from Churchill. I never found the season so dreary before; but this happy meeting will make us young again. Frederica runs much in my thoughts, and when Reginald has recovered his usual good spirits (as I trust he soon will), we will try to rob him of his heart once more, and I am full of hopes of seeing their hands joined at no great distance.

Your affectionate mother
C. DE COURCY

LETTER 41

Mrs. Vernon to Lady De Courcy

Churchill

My dear Madam

Your letter has surprised me beyond measure! Can it be true that they are really separated—and for ever? I should be over-joyed if I dared depend on it, but after all that I have seen, how can one be secure? And Reginald really with you! My surprise is the greater because on Wednesday, the very day of his coming to Parklands, we had a most unexpected and unwelcome visit from Lady Susan, looking all chearfulness and good-humour, and seeming more as if she were to marry him when she got to London, than as if parted from him forever. She staid nearly two hours, was as affectionate and agreable as ever, and not a sylla-ble, not a hint, was dropped of any disagreement or coolness between them. I asked her whether she had seen my brother since his arrival in Town—not, as you may suppose, with any doubt of the fact—but merely to see how she looked. She immediately answered, without any embarrassment, that he had been kind enough to call on her on Monday, but she beleived he had already returned home—which I was very far from crediting.

Your kind invitation is accepted by us with pleasure, and on Thursday next we and our little ones will be with you. Pray Heaven! Reginald may not be in Town again by that time.

I wish we could bring dear Frederica too, but I am sorry to say that her mother's errand hither was to fetch her away; and, miserable as it made the poor girl, it was impossible to detain her. I was thoroughly unwilling to let her go, and so was her uncle; and all that could be urged we *did* urge; but Lady Susan declared that as she was now about to fix herself in Town for several months, she could not be easy if her daughter were not with her, for masters, etc. Her manner, to be sure, was very kind and proper—and Mr. Vernon beleives that Frederica will now be treated with affection. I wish I could think so too!

The poor girl's heart was almost broke at taking leave of us. I charged her to write to me very often, and to remember that if she were in any distress, we should be always her friends. I took care to see her alone, that I might say all this, and I hope made her a little more comfortable. But I shall not be easy till I can go to Town and judge of her situation myself.

I wish there were a better prospect than now appears of the match which the conclusion of your letter declares your expectation of. At present it is not very likely.

Yours etc.

CATH. VERNON

CONCLUSION

This correspondence, by a meeting between some of the parties, and a separation between the others, could not, to the great detriment of the post office revenue, be continued longer. Very little assistance to the state could be derived from the epistolary intercourse of Mrs. Vernon and her neice; for the former soon perceived, by the style of Frederica's letters, that they were written under her mother's inspection, and therefore deferring all particular inquiry till she could make it personally in Town, ceased writing minutely or often.

Having learnt enough in the meanwhile from her open-hearted brother, of what had passed between him and Lady Susan to sink the latter lower than ever in her opinion, she was proportionably more anxious to get Frederica removed from such a mother, and placed under her own care; and, tho' with little hope of success, was resolved to leave nothing unattempted that might offer a chance of obtaining her sister-in-law's consent to it. Her anxiety on the subject made her press for an early visit to London; and Mr. Vernon, who, as it must already have appeared, lived only to do whatever he was desired, soon found some accommodating business to call him thither. With a heart full of the matter, Mrs. Vernon waited on Lady Susan shortly after her arrival in Town, and was met with such an easy and chearful affection, as made her almost turn from her with horror. No remembrance of Reginald, no consciousness of guilt, gave one look of embarrassment. She was in excellent spirits, and seemed eager to shew at once, by every possible attention to her brother and sister, her sense of their kindness, and her pleasure in their society.

Frederica was no more altered than Lady Susan; the same restrained manners, the same timid look in the presence of her mother as heretofore, assured her aunt of her situation's being uncomfortable, and confirmed her in the plan of altering it. No unkindness, however, on the part of Lady Susan appeared. Persecution on the subject of Sir James was entirely at an end—his name merely mentioned to say that he was not in London; and indeed, in all her conversation she was solicitous only for the welfare and improvement of her daughter, acknowledging in terms of grateful delight that Frederica was now growing every day more and more what a parent could desire.

Mrs. Vernon, surprised and incredulous, knew not what to suspect, and, without any change in her own views, only feared greater difficulty in accomplishing them. The first hope of anything better was derived from Lady Susan's asking her whether she thought Frederica looked quite as well as she had done at

Churchill, as she must confess herself to have sometimes an anxious doubt of London's perfectly agreeing with her.

Mrs. Vernon, encouraging the doubt, directly proposed her neice's returning with them into the country. Lady Susan was unable to express her sense of such kindness, yet knew not, from a variety of reasons, how to part with her daughter; and as, tho' her own plans were not yet wholly fixed, she trusted it would ere long be in her power to take Frederica into the country herself, concluded by declining entirely to profit by such unexampled attention. Mrs. Vernon, however, persevered in the offer of it; and tho' Lady Susan continued to resist, her resistance in the course of a few days seemed somewhat less formidable.

The lucky alarm of an influenza decided what might not have been decided quite so soon. Lady Susan's maternal fears were then too much awakened for her to think of anything but Frederica's removal from the risk of infection. Above all disorders in the world, she most dreaded the influenza for her daughter's constitution. Frederica returned to Churchill with her uncle and aunt; and three weeks afterwards, Lady Susan announced her being married to Sir James Martin.

Mrs. Vernon was then convinced of what she had only suspected before, that she might have spared herself all the trouble of urging a removal which Lady Susan had doubtless resolved on from the first. Frederica's visit was nominally for six weeks; but her mother, tho' inviting her to return in one or two affectionate letters, was very ready to oblige the whole party by consenting to a prolongation of her stay, and in the course of two months ceased to write of her absence, and in the course of two more to write to her at all.

Frederica was therefore fixed in the family of her uncle and aunt till such time as Reginald De Courcy could be talked, flattered, and finessed into an affection for her—which, allowing leisure for the conquest of his attachment to her mother, for his abjuring all future attachments, and detesting the sex, might be reasonably looked for in the course of a twelvemonth. Three months might have done it in general, but Reginald's feelings were no less lasting than lively.

Whether Lady Susan was or was not happy in her second

choice—I do not see how it can ever be ascertained—for who would take her assurance of it on either side of the question? The world must judge from probability; she had nothing against her but her husband and her conscience.

Sir James may seem to have drawn a harder lot than mere folly merited. I leave him, therefore, to all the pity that anybody can give him. For myself, I confess that *I* can pity only Miss Manwaring, who, coming to Town and putting herself to an expense in cloathes, which impoverished her for two years, on purpose to secure him, was defrauded of her due by a woman ten years older than herself.